There were smells in here. Curious smells from every direction, smells she couldn't quite identify. Like the one lingering upon her blanket and in the tangled strands of her hair . . . an outdoor smell: wild and earthy, and not altogether unpleasant. It reminded her of frost and snowy moonlight, autumn wind, and warm, wet fur . . .

Oh my God, what's happening?

Trembling violently, she eased the blanket down from her shoulders. Her skin felt raw against the roughness of the fabric, raw and chilled and unusually sensitive. To her shock, she suddenly realized that all her clothes had been removed.

Lucy curled herself tightly beneath the blanket. *Please let this be a dream—please let me wake up!* Her mind was wild with terror, her heart pumped out of control. She couldn't breathe, couldn't stop shaking, couldn't stop the frantic spinning of her thoughts. Where was she and how had she gotten here?

A dank breeze snaked across the floor, threatening the candlelight and swathing Lucy in those strange and secret smells. But there was another odor she detected now—a much stronger odor than the one she'd noticed before. Something dead. Something spoiled . . .

The Unseen

part 2

rest in peace

RICHIE TANKERSLEY CUSICK

speak

An Imprint of Penguin Group (USA) Inc.

For Sandra, Barbara, Julie, Susan, Jenifer, Anna,
Suzanne, Janice, Ellen, Peggy, Richard, Pete, and
Bill—I could never make it through these writing
days without you. Thanks with all my heart.

SPEAK
Published by the Penguin Group
Penguin Group (USA) Inc., 345 Hudson Street, New York, New York 10014, U.S.A.
Penguin Group (Canada), 90 Eglinton Avenue East, Suite 700, Toronto, Ontario, Canada M4P 2Y3
(a division of Pearson Penguin Canada Inc.)
Penguin Books Ltd, 80 Strand, London WC2R 0RL, England
Penguin Ireland, 25 St Stephen's Green, Dublin 2, Ireland
(a division of Penguin Books Ltd)
Penguin Group (Australia), 250 Camberwell Road, Camberwell, Victoria 3124, Australia
(a division of Pearson Australia Group Pty Ltd)
Penguin Books India Pvt Ltd, 11 Community Centre, Panchsheel Park,
New Delhi - 110 017, India
Penguin Group (NZ), Cnr Airborne and Rosedale Roads, Albany, Auckland 1310, New Zealand (a
division of Pearson New Zealand Ltd)
Penguin Books (South Africa) (Pty) Ltd, 24 Sturdee Avenue, Rosebank,
Johannesburg 2196, South Africa

Registered Offices: Penguin Books Ltd, 80 Strand, London WC2R 0RL, England

First published in the UK by Scholastic Ltd, 2004
Published by Speak, an imprint of Penguin Group (USA) Inc., 2005

1 3 5 7 9 10 8 6 4 2

Copyright © Richie Tankersley Cusick, 2004

LIBRARY OF CONGRESS CATALOGING-IN-PUBLICATION DATA
Cusick, Richie Tankersley.
Rest in peace / Richie Tankersley Cusick.
p.   cm. – (The unseen ; pt. 2)
First published in the UK by Scholastic Ltd., 2004.
Summary: Having survived the accident that killed her friend Byron, Lucy tries to cope with
her new powers and attempts to figure out who—or what—is stalking her.
ISBN: 0-14-240464-0 (pbk.)
[1. Extrasensory perception—Fiction.   2. Horror stories—Fiction.] I. Title.
PZ7.C9646Res 2005 [Fic]—dc22 2005047435

Printed in the United States of America

Prologue

He stood and he watched her.

Watched the frantic rolling of her eyes beneath her closed, bruised eyelids . . . the terrified heaving of her breasts beneath the torn, mangled material of her blouse. From time to time a whimper escaped her lips . . . or a gasp . . . or even a whispered plea for help, as she dreamed her terrible dream. And sometimes her hands would thrash against the darkness, clawing at shadows and bloodstained bandages, as she relived, over and over again, those last tragic moments of her waking nightmare . . .

He knew this dream well.

Knew every scene—every gory, meticulous detail—for he had been with her the night it began, and he had been with her every night since, feeling it replay endlessly, torturously, through her sleep . . .

So this is what it's like to die . . .

Lying there on her back in the grass, all alone in the darkness, Lucy could sense the wet, runny mask of her face. Tears? Blood? She couldn't be sure, couldn't be sure she even had a face, couldn't be sure about anything except that her body screamed in pain each time she tried to draw even the shallowest of breaths.

I can't move . . . Help . . . Somebody, help me . . .

With a ragged cry, Lucy tried to lift her head, tried to peer through the thick, endless night surrounding her. As in a dream, she could see the faraway sky blazing bright, lit by a giant fire—and along with those sickening smells of pain and fear and despair that threatened to choke her, now there was the gasoline . . . burning rubber . . . white-hot metal . . . and something else . . . something dear to her heart . . .

Byron!

That's Byron's van!

She'd been sitting in the front seat beside him, and she'd been staring at the moon. That blood red moon hovering there behind the trees and glowing out through the dark, shredded fabric of the clouds. She'd been staring at the moon, and then she'd jolted with the first sharp swerve of the van. Confused and groggy, she'd heard Byron's shout, the piercing shriek of brakes and tires, she'd felt the road give way to air beneath them as they dove off the shoulder and off the crest of the hill, and out through the foggy night, plummeting down and down into nothingness . . .

Byron? Can you hear me?

She knew somehow that she hadn't spoken aloud, knew somehow that her thoughts had burst free of her pain, only to fall silent among the shadows. It was so dark out here. So dark, so frighteningly still, except for those flames leaping and glowing against the distant horizon . . .

Something ran in front of us.

With a moan, Lucy struggled to shut out the pain, struggled to focus her hazy thoughts.

Byron tried to swerve, he tried to miss hitting it, but something ran in front of us . . .

She wished she could remember. She wished she could remember what it was that had caused the accident. But there was only the briefest glimmer of memory in that last fatal second, only the briefest

3

image of something caught in the headlights as the car veered and left the road.

What was that?

It seemed so familiar somehow . . .

But her thoughts were fading . . . fading . . . and she knew she was slipping away. In desperation she stared up at the trees overhead, great gnarled branches etched thickly against the black dome of the sky. And then she noticed that moon.

So full and round. So red like blood. Caught in a web of tangled limbs, oozing out through the clouds, wine stains on velvet.

Byron, I'm so scared! Please help me!

And that's when she heard it.

The soft rustling sound, like wind sighing through grass. Except that she couldn't feel any wind, not even the faintest of breezes, in this heavy night air.

The sound was close by.

Coming even closer . . .

Oh God!

Once more she tried to lift herself, to call out for help. But the rustlings were in her head now, in her thoughts and in her pain, like so many urgent whispers, whispers of great importance.

As Lucy's head turned helplessly to one side, she saw

shadows all around her, shadows slinking along the ground and through the trees, slivers of black and pale pale gray, and sparks of amber light . . .

Terror exploded within her. Even through the paralyzing numbness of pain and shock, she sensed that these were animals, and she sensed why they were here. Instinct told her that she was surrounded, though one stood closer than the others. She could hear the slow, calm rhythm of its breathing as it watched her from a place she couldn't see.

Oh, God, don't let me die like this!

She thought of Byron. The vision burst inside her brain with such force that she choked and gagged and vomited blood in the grass. In that one instant of agonizing clarity she saw his midnight eyes, heard his calm, deep voice telling her not to be afraid. Now she remembered how he'd turned to her in that last split second of his life, his eyes desperate with helplessness and disbelief as he'd reached for her hand. Did he touch me? *The thought drifted through her mind, light as a feather.* Did we touch one last time?

But the whispers were louder now, and the fire was brighter than ever, and she was so weak . . . so tired.

Please . . . please . . . just let me die fast . . .

Night swayed around her. As tears ran silently

down her cheeks, something huge and dark leaned in over her, blocking her view of the sky.

She braced herself for the end. Felt hot breath caressing her throat . . . smelled the faint, familiar scent of something sweet . . .

Byron . . . I'm so sorry . . .

"Byron has gone," the voice murmured. "Only I can save you now."

Down, down, she sank . . . into the endlessness of time . . .

Who are you . . . ? What are you . . . ?

And that voice . . . fading far into nothingness. . .

"Oh, Lucy . . . there's no name for what we are . . ."

And so he stood, and he watched her.

How lovely she was . . . and how curious . . . so small and fragile, her pale skin nearly transparent, her expression as remote, as beautiful, as death.

But not quite.

Not quite dead yet.

Shock was just a stepping-stone. It would be so easy, he knew, to ease her across that tenuous threshold; just one swift, silent act on his part.

But there was something entrancing . . . mesmerizing . . . about the way she hovered there—just on the edge, between life and eternity—that was exciting to him.

There had been no time to take her before.

Before, as he dragged her to safety, and then as she lay there in the tall scorched grass, bruised and battered and drenched in blood, the others sweeping in silently around her, quivering with anticipation . . .

But "No," he had ordered them. "Stand away—this one is mine."

Damn those who had stopped to help!

And a firetruck, no less—a whole *convoy* of emergency vehicles, in fact—heading homeward from some tragedy, following a careful distance behind the van, yet still close enough to witness its fatal careen off the road, its hurtling descent down the rocky hillside, the bits and pieces of its broken shell raining like fireworks through the shattered night.

So many people! Sirens, lights, confusion!

The others of his kind had fled at once, but he alone had stayed.

He alone had stayed behind . . .

Hidden and silent . . .

Guarding his prize.

So there had been no time to take her then, in the panic, the chaos, of that hopeless rescue, the air stinking of futility and death even as he swept her away with him through the fog-shrouded woods, to this place of dark secrets and solitude. And every night afterward . . . including this late night . . . he had been here, watching over her, slinking through the terror of her dreams.

It was these dreams he feasted on in the meantime.

The loneliness, the heartache, the empty black holes of despair.

Hazy images of a mother who had died . . . a cozy home that was no more . . . and now this loss of someone new, this grievous, unexpected loss of Byron . . . such painful memories buried within her, buried deep, because to remember them would be far too much agony to endure.

"Cold . . . I'm so cold . . ."

He heard her whimper, a plea as faint as breath. And there was no hesitation as he leaned down over her, his lips drawn instinctively to that perfect, most sensitive spot.

Relief was instant and needle-sharp—teeth stabbing like fire, piercing hot through her skin, sinking deep through her flesh, clamping down and holding on, suspending her on boiling waves of panic and burning pleasure . . .

"*Lucy . . .*" His breath caressed her cheek, the delicate lids of her eyes, the tender flesh of her throat . . . "*No more cold . . . no more pain . . . no more loneliness . . .*"

Had she smiled? Ever so softly in her sleep?

He pondered this as he gazed upon her, as she stirred languidly in the aftermath of his kiss. Pondered this so intently that he failed to anticipate the slight, sudden movement of her hand as it groped through the shadows and brushed the side of his face, touching him with an innocence that caught him completely unaware.

He drew in his breath, every muscle tightening. His keen eyes narrowed, gleaming with annoyance and a hint of wonder. He had let his guard down—a weakness he could not afford—and yet for that one fleeting second, the gentle reward of her hand upon his cheek had been well worth his carelessness.

He drew back from her now, strangely unnerved, as her hand lowered once again to her side. As she lay weak and helpless, lost in the sorrow of her memories.

But little by little he would take those memories.

Devour them until the past, as she knew it, existed no more.

And then she would be filled with him . . . her mind, her body, her soul.

Like life's rich blood . . .

Filled with him and him alone.

1

Lucy's eyes flew open.

With a gasp of terror, she tried to scream, to fight her way free, but *free from what*, she wondered groggily, *I can't move, I can't see, something's holding me down* . . .

"Aunt Irene?"

She'd meant to call out, yet she couldn't hear her own voice. There was only silence, as still and deep as a grave, and the frantic pounding of her heartbeat.

"Aunt Irene, are you there?"

Slowly . . . hazily . . . her surroundings began shifting into focus. Lucy realized that she was lying on her back, and that the thing holding her down was a blanket—a blanket that should have been easy to push back, except that she didn't have the strength to kick it away. Beneath her the ground was cold and damp; beside her a candle flickered weakly, its melted stub drowning in a puddle of wax. As she gazed up at the curved ceiling, grotesque shadows leaped across in a macabre dance.

Where am I?

There were smells in here. Curious smells from every direction, smells she couldn't quite identify. Like the one lingering upon her blanket and in the tangled strands of her hair . . . an outdoors smell, wild and earthy, and not altogether unpleasant. It reminded her of frost and snowy moonlight, autumn wind and warm, wet fur . . .

A musky smell. A primitive smell.

Some sort of animal?

Moaning softly, Lucy struggled to sit up, totally unprepared for the wave of dizziness that pulled her down again. Her whole body reeled from the force of it; her nerves screamed in agony as pain ripped through every bone and muscle. Clutching her head with both hands, she felt a strip of wet, sticky cloth sagging low over her left eye.

"Aunt Irene!"

A spray of stars burst in her brain. It blurred behind her eyes, and memories began struggling to the surface of her mind, clawing their way through a sludge of fear and rising panic.

Byron! Oh, God, I remember . . . I remember everything. The accident . . . fire . . . and he didn't get out . . . Byron didn't get out—

"Can anyone hear me?" Lucy cried. "Please! Is anybody there?"

Oh my God, what's happening?

Trembling violently, she eased the blanket down from her shoulders. Her skin felt raw against the roughness of the fabric, raw and chilled and unusually sensitive. To her shock, she suddenly realized that all her clothes had been removed.

Lucy curled herself tightly beneath the blanket. *Please let this be a dream—please let me wake up!* Her mind was wild with terror, her heart pumped out of control. She couldn't breathe, couldn't stop shaking, couldn't stop the frantic spinning of her thoughts. Where was she, and how had she gotten here? How badly was she injured? How long had she been unconscious, and who had been here with her while she'd slept? She had to get away—*run* away—but from what? From whom? And where would she go? How could she possibly escape from one unknown to another?

And then a much more chilling thought crept in among all the others. Was someone here with her right now? Watching as she realized her hopeless predicament? Waiting for her to make a move? Cat and mouse, waiting to pounce?

Without warning, the ground gave a slow, deep shudder beneath her. As Lucy cried out in alarm, she felt another rumble of thunder resonating through the shadows; she heard the muffled, but unmistakable, downpouring of rain.

A storm. And it sounded close by.

Clenching her teeth against another onslaught of pain, Lucy reached out for the candle. She pried it from the glaze of dried wax, then held it at arm's length, moving it in a slow, deliberate arc.

She seemed to be in a cave. A small, denlike space with damp, water-stained walls and a low ceiling. About fifteen feet off to her left, the ceiling vanished completely into the pitch-blackness of a tunnel—while the same distance to her right, it sloped sharply upward before dead-ending.

No . . . not a dead end . . .

As Lucy's gaze followed the angle of the ceiling, she realized it led to an opening—a tiny opening scarcely big enough to squeeze through, an opening she hadn't recognized at first because it was covered up. But now she could see a hint of gray light around its edges, and a ragged hole near the bottom where part of the camouflage had blown away, and she realized that tree branches had been stacked up and wedged in from outside.

Someone had deliberately disguised the entrance to the cave.

To keep others out?

Or to keep me in?

A dank breeze snaked across the floor, threatening the candlelight and swathing Lucy in those strange and secret smells. But there was another odor she detected now—a much stronger odor than the one she'd noticed before. Something dead. Something spoiled.

Only bats, she tried to convince herself. Bats and rats and other creepy things that hid in dark places, shying away from the light. Or some wounded animal that had wandered in here once upon a time to die. Some poor creature, lost and trapped.

Trapped like me.

With sheer willpower, Lucy pulled herself to her knees. The feeble candlelight revealed several small puddles of water around her—black, shiny pools, shallow but thick. She could see dark splatters over the ground, and dark smears trailing back into the tunnel where her light couldn't reach.

She drew in her breath and closed her eyes. She opened them again and swallowed down a sick taste of fear.

Clutching the blanket, Lucy worked her way slowly to the nearest wall. It took several moments for her queasiness to pass, even longer to stand up. The gloom spun around her as she braced against the stone. She forced herself to take three halting steps.

There was no time to lose.

Moving toward the front of the cave, Lucy

spotted a pile of clothes lying directly in her path. She picked it up and ran her fingertips through the tangled shreds, relief giving way to disappointment. Her blouse—or rather, what was left of it—was completely useless. Her jacket was there, too—torn and stained, with one sleeve ripped away, but at least it was dry. Her jeans were missing. Also her socks. No shoes. No underwear.

Lucy eased her arms slowly, torturously, into her jacket. Then once again she wrapped the blanket around her shoulders and started walking.

Keep going. You can do it. One step at a time . . .

Her foot sank into something wet.

Wet and cold and slimy.

At once a stench rose into the air, the same foul odor she'd smelled before, except it was overpowering now, *suffocating* now. She jerked away, wiping her foot across the ground, and in the weakening candlelight saw one of the thick, black puddles she'd stepped in. She stumbled back, only to realize that the hem of her blanket had also trailed in the pool. Quickly she yanked it up again, losing her balance as her other foot slammed down on something small and furry.

She felt the sharp snap of tiny bones.

The gush of curdled liquid squishing between her toes.

Screaming, Lucy toppled over, landing hard on her stomach, fighting desperately not to pass out. As she lifted her head, she found herself staring into the dull, sightless eyes of a rabbit.

It had been dead for quite a while.

She could tell from the lolling posture of its neck, the jagged slash through its underbelly, the way it had been savagely gutted, leaving only a few strings of raw flesh and muscle and leftover entrails smeared across the bottom of her foot.

Lucy's mind went dark.

As her fingers dug into the ground, the whole world turned upside down, and her brain exploded in a kaleidoscope of panic:

Running—racing—right left zigzag path—paws thundering silently—shadow swift—scent of hopeless terror—screams—shrill screams—breath razor hot—sprays of red gurgling bubbling—

One last look at the sky . . . one last smell of the pines . . . sweet woodland home fading . . .

Lucy's eyes slowly opened. Shaking violently, she turned her head sideways and threw up.

The candle flared one last time.

As Lucy tried to reach it, to revive it for another second, the hot red wax dripped over her fingers, molding to her like a second skin.

As though her own hand was stained with the innocent blood of her vision.

2

It was madness, she knew.

Sheer madness to run, not knowing where she was or what lay outside the cave, not knowing where she could possibly go.

Sheer, utter madness.

Yet not nearly as crazy as staying here, Lucy reminded herself. Here in this place of death and darkness, not knowing when her captor might return. She knew now that those pools and splatters on the ground, those stains leading back into the tunnel, could be only one thing— and that much blood could never have come from one small rabbit.

What kind of person was she dealing with?

What kind of insanity?

Peeling the wax from her fingers, Lucy staggered to her feet and limped to the entrance of the cave. Her earlier suspicions had been right—someone had tried to cover it with brush and branches, but where some of the limbs had fallen away, she had a clear view of the world beyond.

Trees.

Trees as far as she could see. A leaden gray sky overhead. Ghostly gray mist . . . a solid downpour of cold gray rain. Lucy couldn't tell if it was dusk or early morning.

He could be out there right now. Hiding. Watching. Waiting to see if I'll try to escape. Waiting so he can catch me and bring me back again.

It was a chance she had to take.

Steeling herself, she began tearing at the barricade. The branches were heavy and cumbersome, most of them hopelessly entwined, and Lucy had to stop frequently to catch her breath, brace herself against the wall, will her dizziness away, and force herself not to cry out. The blanket slipped from her shoulders onto the wet ground. The few remaining buttons on her jacket were useless against the chill. Every simple movement was almost more than she could bear.

But at last she began to make headway. The opening grew larger; she could see more of the woods beyond. The rain fell harder, and as she stopped once more to catch her breath, she gathered the soggy blanket and shoved it through the opening. *Not much protection, but better than nothing.* She watched it land in a puddle on the other side, and then, gathering all the strength she could, Lucy squeezed through after it.

The ground was frozen. The wind was raw. Her whole body recoiled from the shock of the elements, and for several agonizing moments all she could do was lie there, sprawled in the mud where she'd fallen. Something slid down over her left eye, and she managed to pull it off. She remembered feeling a strip of cloth there earlier. Now she could see that it was a bandage, and that it was soaked with blood.

My blood? Oh God . . . how bad am I really hurt?

With cautious fingers she touched the swollen places on her forehead, the ragged edges of split skin, the crustiness in her hair. She choked down a fresh wave of horror and stumbled to her feet, then pulled the blanket around her and began to run.

She had no idea where she was going. She simply plunged into the woods, ignoring the dizziness in her head, the weakness in her knees. Her body felt like a stranger's body as she tried to drag it through the forest, tripping over the soggy blanket, crawling through the mud and underbrush, forcing herself up again. She could see her breath—short gasps of pain hanging frosty in the air—and her nose was running, and her tears seemed to freeze upon her cheeks. Her heart thudded in her ears, and every clumsy footstep seemed to echo around her, causing her to look back in terror, certain she was being followed.

Don't stop—run! Run faster, run harder! Run for your life!

But run *where*?

Lucy was completely lost. Like a liquid dream, minutes flowed into hours, and then into no time at all. The woods were endless. With so many twists and turns, she wondered if she might even be going in circles. It was definitely growing darker. She couldn't feel her feet anymore. As she glanced down to see if they were still at the end of her legs, she realized that the blanket had fallen off, though she didn't remember dropping it.

It doesn't matter! Keep running!

She tried to hold her jacket around her, but her arms had gone numb. Through the steady rush of rain, she was aware of trees like phantoms, and the dying brilliance of fallen leaves, thick cushions of pine needles, and the ups and downs of hills that went on and on.

She wanted to give up.

To collapse and simply lie there, to close her eyes and drift away.

Better to die out here than back in the cave. Better to die on her own terms than at the hands of some maniac.

She paused a moment, breath sharp in her ribs, trying to peer off through the dense maze of trees. Surely there was a house out here somewhere—a farm, a cabin? Surely there must be a pathway or a road? She thought about screaming for help, but decided against it. She doubted anyone could hear her above this rain, and if her captor had returned by now to find her missing, she couldn't take the chance of giving herself away.

Lucy turned slowly in all directions.

There must be a way out—there *had* to be a way out!

And then her body went rigid with fear.

A shadow?

Had she seen a shadow just now . . . off to the side of her . . . slipping through the woods?

Seconds crept by but she couldn't move, could scarcely even breathe. Of course she'd imagined it. The rain was playing tricks on her. It was just leaves swirling to the ground, branches swaying in the wind, some startled animal taking cover between the trees.

That's all it is, Lucy. That's all.

Rallying her courage, she forced herself to go on. Then stopped again, almost immediately.

She *hadn't* imagined it—she was sure this time!

A dark silhouette through the foggy rain, just a glimpse as it glided up the incline about twenty yards away, then vanished behind some rocks.

Lucy's heart ricocheted into her throat. A

bear? Yet it seemed too graceful, too fast to be a bear. And the vague, unsettling shape of it . . . something so dangerous . . .

So familiar . . .

The low stone wall behind Irene's house . . . the woods, the deserted road at the Fall Festival . . . the large, murky figure darting in front of Byron's van . . .

"Oh God," Lucy whispered. "Oh God, please help me!"

In sheer panic she began to run. Mindless now with terror, exhausted beyond reason, she stumbled deeper and deeper under cover of the forest, never even noticing the sudden glimmer of light just ahead of her. As Lucy plunged through the trees, the ground disappeared without warning.

There was a dreamlike sensation of falling, of floating, before she suddenly slammed back to reality and rolled down the side of the hill. The earth was soft where she landed, but her body screamed on impact. She lay there, too stunned to move, her breath completely jolted out of her. Against her icy cheeks, the flow of blood felt warm and almost comforting.

Cautiously, Lucy tried to lift her head. She was lying in tall dead weeds, and as she moaned softly and squinted through her pain, she imagined she could see a dirt road not five feet away.

Her head fell back again. She closed her eyes against the rain and tasted blood trickling into the corners of her mouth.

And then she heard a sound.

A sound like an engine, like a car.

Tears came to her eyes, and she pinched the skin on her arm, pinched it hard to make herself wake up, because she knew she couldn't bear one more nightmare, one more disappointment.

But the sound was still there.

And it was coming closer.

With her last ounce of strength, Lucy dragged herself onto the road. She tried to lift one arm, tried to give a feeble wave as the car bore down on her. She knew the driver probably couldn't see her through the rain, through the dusk, and as the headlights blinded her, she braced herself for the shock.

There was a loud squeal of brakes, a wet skid of tires.

And then a door opening . . . hands on her shoulders, turning her over, rearranging her jacket, smoothing back her hair.

Arms lifted her. Carried her without the slightest effort, then settled her gently onto the backseat.

And then, as she finally surrendered to blissful unconsciousness, Lucy heard soft words whispered through the dark.

"Remember to look both ways, Lucy. It's a dangerous road you're on."

3

"My meeting will probably run late tonight, Lucy. Will you be all right here alone?"

Startled, Lucy glanced up to see her aunt standing in the living room doorway. With one quick movement, Lucy managed to hide the piece of paper she'd been holding, slipping it underneath some magazines stacked beside her on the couch.

"I'll be fine." Lucy forced a smile, even though her heart gave a sickening clench. *Of course I'll be fine, I'm used to it; even when you are here, I'm still alone.* But still, she couldn't keep from asking, "Are you sure everything's locked?"

"The house is completely secure, I've told you before. And I'll set the alarm on my way out."

But it didn't matter *how* many times Irene had told her, Lucy never felt entirely protected, never entirely safe. She merely *pretended* each time to be reassured by her aunt's promises, because she knew Irene would never believe her if she told the truth. Neither Irene nor anyone else would ever believe that something, or someone, was after Lucy. Sometimes Lucy wasn't even sure she believed it herself, yet the nagging dread was always there, like a shadow over her shoulder.

And anyway, Lucy told herself, *where else could I go?*

Her aunt turned to leave, hesitated, then faced her again. *Like a robot*, Lucy thought, *more cold and withdrawn than ever*. As though Angela's disappearance had added a final layer of distance to those steel barriers around Irene's heart. Lucy couldn't help wondering how differently things might have turned out if that relationship between stepmother and stepdaughter hadn't been so strained. But speculations were pointless, and now she watched curiously as her aunt's lips twisted into a tight semblance of a smile.

"Did Dr. Fielding mention your going back to school?" she asked, and Lucy nodded.

"Yes. On Monday."

"He feels it's best for you to get back into a normal routine. I agree with him."

Of course you do. Out of sight, out of mind.

"He called me this afternoon." Irene seemed to be struggling for conversation. "He says you're doing well. He says you're coming to terms." Another uncomfortable pause, and then she straightened. "You should eat. Fix yourself something in the microwave. There's pizza. Angela always . . ."

Abruptly her aunt walked away. Lucy waited for the sound of the back door to close, then jumped up and went systematically around the house, checking windows, double-checking that shades were drawn and curtains were closed, inspecting locks and deadbolts and the security system. Then, as satisfied as she could be that the house was impregnable, she sat down again and pulled out the paper she'd hidden.

Angela, Lucy thought miserably, *where are you?* She stared down at the crumpled poster. A poster of Angela, just like the ones she'd seen plastered all over town.

With a weary sigh, Lucy snuggled deep into the couch and leaned her head back against the cushions. No one had seen or heard from Angela since that Saturday night of the festival, the night of Lucy and Byron's accident, that strange and fatal night just over a week ago.

Things like this don't happen. How many times had Lucy told herself that in the days following the tragedies? *Things like this happen only in movies. Happen only to strangers. Things like this don't happen in real life, not to normal people.*

But I'm not normal anymore, she had to remind herself now for at least the hundredth time. Not since she'd wandered into the cemetery that night and found Katherine. No matter how much she tried to pretend, nothing would ever be the same again, and it had taken Byron to convince her of that.

Byron . . .

She'd cried buckets of tears, cried until she couldn't cry anymore. The guilt was more than she could bear—the doubts, the regrets, replaying those last moments of Byron's life.

Her heart and soul felt empty. So empty, in fact, that she often found herself wondering if maybe *she* had died, too, and that this strange half existence was but a lingering dream. Her salvation had become a cold sort of numbness, a distancing of herself from both memories and emotions. This was the only way she'd been able to survive.

The only way she would *ever* be able to survive.

Reaching over, Lucy lifted a mug of cocoa from the end table, then tested the foamy marshmallows with her tongue. The chocolate was sweet and hot, but did little to warm the chill inside her. As she took a cautious sip, her gaze returned to the small poster she'd placed in her lap.

MISSING: HAVE YOU SEEN ANGELA?

Looking back at her was a color-copy image of Angela's face, taken from her senior class photo. Those perfect cheekbones and flowing black hair, that model-perfect smile. *I wonder where that smile is now? I wonder if she even can smile?*

Lucy fought off the familiar waves of guilt and set her mug back on the table. Then she put the poster aside, drew both knees up to her chin, and wrapped her arms tight around them.

"Not your fault," Dr. Fielding would say if he could share her thoughts now. "Circumstances beyond your control," he'd remind her, and "You can't keep torturing yourself."

Good old Dr. Fielding. Aunt Irene's personal choice of prominent friends, who was supposed to be helping Lucy through the nightmares, helping her to readjust, helping her to come to terms with all that had happened.

Except Dr. Fielding didn't know the half of it. And Lucy knew she could never tell him.

"It's only been a week, Lucy," the doctor had reminded her in their session just that afternoon. "These things take time. Often, quite a lot of time."

And Lucy had given her dutiful nod and tried to listen politely. Because how could Dr. Fielding even *begin* to have a clue as to what she was going through? How could she even *begin* to tell him everything that had happened to her since she'd first come to Pine Ridge?

"Like I explained to you in the hospital, you

might experience dizziness or light-headedness—possibly fainting spells. You may become disoriented or suffer memory lapses. There could be flashbacks pertaining to the accident, or you might even experience panic attacks."

"Great," Lucy had responded. "That certainly gives me something to look forward to."

But Dr. Fielding had smiled his kind smile and patted her on the shoulder. "These occurrences are all very common with a head injury, Lucy—nothing to be overly concerned about. The important thing is to accept the fact that even if they *do* happen, you really are okay. And you really *are* going to get better."

"But you still think I made everything up."

She'd watched his face, that carefully controlled doctor face, as he'd steepled his fingers beneath his chin and studied her from his leather chair.

"I think that trauma-induced memories are very tricky things," he'd answered, as she'd known he would.

"I'm not lying about what happened."

"I know you're not lying. I believe that *you* believe everything you've told me. And it's still

35

amazing to *everyone* how you could have survived that accident, much less survived for three days afterward."

Lucy's hands had twisted in her lap. "I told you. I was in a cave. But I don't know how I got there."

"And those are three days and nights still unaccounted for," he'd sighed. "The police didn't even know you'd been with Byron until your aunt came home the next day and reported you and Angela missing. And even then, it took time to track down witnesses at the Festival who saw you and Byron leave together. After that, search parties combed that entire area around the accident site. Hundreds of people, even scent dogs, spread out for miles. No one discovered a cave. There wasn't a house or a trail or a single clue. But you must have found shelter somehow, somewhere. It's a total mystery. And nothing short of a miracle."

Lucy had heard it all before. She'd told the police everything she could remember about her ordeal—the muffled sounds and shadows, the pools of blood, the dead rabbit, how someone had tried to camouflage the entrance to the cave, and how she'd finally escaped in spite of it. She'd told the doctors, too, and Aunt Irene, and even the private investigator her aunt had hired to search for Angela. But she knew they didn't believe her. Like Dr. Fielding, they all thought she suffered from delusions, the results of her head injury, exposure, and shock.

"But someone found me and brought me to the hospital," she couldn't help reminding him. "And that was real."

Dr. Fielding had conceded with a smile. "Yes. That was definitely real. Three days after the accident, someone left you outside the door of the emergency room. No one saw this person come or go, and no one's been able to find out who it was. If they could, it might help enormously in solving your disappearance."

"I just wish I could thank him. I think of him every day, and I try so hard to remember something about him . . . *anything* about him."

"Maybe you're trying too hard."

"All I know is, he wasn't the one in the cave."

"And how can you be so sure?"

"I can't explain it, but I just know. His voice was different."

"Hallucinations can seem very, very real."

Hallucinations? Well, maybe she really *had* imagined it. Maybe she really *was* going insane.

"You remembered drifting in and out of consciousness," Dr. Fielding had said, going over his notes once more. "And the will to survive is an incredible thing. It gives us the endurance we might never have under normal circumstances."

"But what if I'm right? What if I'm right, and whoever I escaped from comes after me again?"

"You're catastrophizing, Lucy. Even if this person *were* real, how could you be any safer than you are right now, with all this attention being focused on you? No one would dare try to kidnap you twice."

Lucy had bitten her lip in frustration. Twisted her hands even tighter in her lap.

"So if I wasn't kidnapped, then what did I do after the wreck? Just wander around for miles and miles? Find shelter in some place that doesn't even exist?"

"There was no serious frostbite on your feet; the hypothermia you suffered was relatively mild. Not nearly severe enough to suggest your wandering outdoors for any extended length of time. Your other injuries were consistent with those from a car accident, or from falling down a hill, as you described—scrapes, bruises, mild concussion, those nasty gashes on your head. No broken bones, incredibly. And the rest of the examination showed no evidence what-soever of any sexual molestation."

Lucy had turned her head away, and stared out the office window. *But someone took my clothes. And someone touched me. And something stung like fire, something I've never felt before . . .*

She still remembered the sensation. Remembered it all too clearly, though she hadn't been able to find any unusual marks on her skin; no tell-tale punctures, no secret scars, nothing intimate or the least bit intrusive. Yet a few times it had come back to her in the middle of the night, in writhing dreams, flushing her entire body with heat and a sense of perpetual emptiness.

Just remembering it in Dr. Fielding's office today had caused that strange, unsettling ache deep, deep within her. An untreatable ache that made her squirm restlessly in her chair.

"I'm very pleased with your test results," the

doctor had continued, not seeming to notice her sudden uneasiness. "Your stitches can come out in a week or two; your soreness, I'm afraid, will take a little longer. And I expect you to make even more progress in the days to come. But injuries take time to heal, you know." His gaze was one of genuine sympathy. "Not just the physical ones, but the emotional ones, as well."

The ache inside her had suddenly focused on her heart.

"You want me to talk about Byron," she said quietly.

"I understand his funeral is this weekend."

Lucy had swallowed tears, barely able to answer. "Tomorrow."

"Are you going to attend?"

But the tears had only thickened as she shook her head. "I can't. There's no way I can do it."

"Do you think it might help give you some sort of closure?"

"How can there ever be closure? I can't stop thinking about him. I can't stop thinking about his grandmother, and how she's going to manage now that he's gone."

"Do you know his grandmother?"

"I've only heard about her. I know she's sick and that Byron took care of her. And I feel so responsible, and I keep thinking how can I possibly help her—"

"Lucy," he'd said, cutting her off gently, "right now you're in no condition to take care of anyone. Right now you need to concentrate on yourself and—"

"Can we just not talk about it anymore?"

There'd been that uncomfortable silence between them then; that silence, Lucy knew, that always preceded some sort of lecture.

At last Dr. Fielding spoke. "I think there are certain things that each of us must work through in our own time, in our own way. Loss and grief are just two of those things. You know I'm always here to help you. Whenever you're ready."

For one split second she'd almost given in. He'd looked so wise, so sincere, that the need to unburden herself had almost been more than she could bear. *Since you're so interested in knowing, Doctor, it all started when I went into the cemetery, found a murdered girl, was touched with a supernatural power, met Byron, and then found myself having weird visions and being watched and followed by some dark shadowy thing . . .*

She'd actually leaned forward. She'd stared into Dr. Fielding's eyes, and her fingers had gripped the arms of her chair.

"When I'm ready," she'd finally answered.

She could tell he'd been disappointed. Yet he'd reached over and given her hand an encouraging squeeze. "With that said, I see no reason why you can't start back to school. I think a normal routine would be very beneficial at this juncture, offer some stability. People your own age . . . fun activities . . . anything to distract you from the terrible ordeal you've just experienced."

"Byron's dead. Angela's missing." These were the words she'd repeated so many, many times that she'd lost count. "It's all my fault."

And once more, Dr. Fielding had given his tireless response. "None of this is your fault, Lucy. None of this was *ever* your fault. Life has its own agenda; it never asks our permission or approval. You're alive, and you're safe. And, believe me . . . that's nothing to feel guilty about."

How simple he made it sound, Lucy thought

now, shifting positions, slumping down on the couch. Had it been only six days since Angela slipped away from the Fall Festival with her invisible boyfriend—generating search parties and volunteers, police investigations and nationwide alerts, false leads and dead-end tips? Lucy could still recall her cousin's behavior that Saturday night—rebellious and excited, mysterious and hopeful with thoughts of love. Now Angela was just another teenage runaway, just another statistic, like millions of other girls that vanished every year.

Except there was nothing typical about Angela's disappearance—Lucy was sure of it. And there was no one—no one at all—whom she could share her suspicions with.

Only Byron.

Byron whose funeral was tomorrow.

Guilt slammed into her with merciless force—the same guilt that battered her day after day, ripping her heart, wearing her down.

"If you want to live," Katherine had told her, *"you mustn't tell anyone what you've seen here tonight."*

The words of the murdered girl echoed

through Lucy's brain. Katherine had warned her that night, and Lucy had chosen to ignore it; Katherine had warned her and died, yet Lucy hadn't really believed.

My fault. I told Byron, I told Byron everything, and now he's dead.

How could she have been so stupid? So irresponsible? How could she have dismissed Katherine's warning so easily?

Because Byron already knew what was happening . . . because Byron already understood the danger . . . because Byron was strong and brave and determined to take a chance . . .

Lucy buried her face in her hands.

She would never escape the guilt. It would never stop tormenting her. And no amount of prayers or tears, no well-meant platitudes or rationalizations, could ever bring Byron back.

She'd felt so horribly alone before.

But that was nothing compared to now.

4

The whole world seemed to be weeping for Byron.

As if in keeping with Lucy's mood, the day dawned gray and bitterly cold. Mist hung thick in the air, and after several feeble attempts to break through, the sun sank despondently behind a mourning veil of clouds.

Lucy closed the sliding glass doors to the balcony. In spite of her warm room and layers of clothes, she dug through her closet and put on another sweatshirt. She hadn't been able to stop shivering since she'd woken up. She'd hardly been able to keep her thoughts straight.

"Are you certain you don't want to go to the funeral?"

Lucy spun around. She hadn't heard Irene in

the hall, and now, as her aunt peered at her from the threshold, Lucy's stomach went queasy. Irene was dressed in conservative black, and her face was completely expressionless.

"I understand he's being buried in the old cemetery, but you needn't go if you feel uncomfortable," the woman went on. "You don't even have to stay for the entire service. Apparently his grandmother requested a casket, but it won't be open, of course, and—"

She broke off, looking uncomfortable.

No open casket, no body, Lucy's guilt taunted her. *Just charred remains*.

"I'm going to be sick," Lucy whispered, and bolted for the bathroom. When she finally came out again, Irene had gone, and a morbid silence settled throughout the house.

For a long while Lucy sat on the edge of her bed. She stared at the clock on her bedside table and watched the slow, torturous passing of time. Less than an hour till Byron's final farewell. Her heartbeat kept time to the tick of the clock. Her chest was so tight, she could hardly breathe. On unsteady legs she went back into the bathroom and stood at the sink, running a cold, wet washcloth over her face.

She looked so pale. Empty and haunted. The way her reflection had looked when Mom died. As though this might be the way she was going to look from now on.

She ran one hand slowly through her long blond hair, wincing at the tiny stitches near her scalp and the ones high up on her forehead. No point using makeup, she decided—nothing could hide the dark smudges beneath her eyes or the hollow expression gazing back at her, and her face would be covered anyway. She wove her hair into a single braid and tucked it down the back of her shirt. Then, returning to her room, she opened the top dresser drawer and took out her jewelry box.

Sadly she gazed down into the jumbled contents. She sifted some tangled necklaces between her fingers, and she sorted through a clump of earrings and silver bracelets. And then she found what she was looking for.

A pin.

A tiny, gold, heart-shaped pin that her mother had given her on her thirteenth birthday.

It had always been special to her, something she'd loved and cherished.

And that's why she wanted Byron to have it now.

Tucking it into her pocket, Lucy hurried downstairs. She went straight to the coat closet in the front hall, where she pulled on an oversized jacket and a pair of thick raglan gloves. She wound a knitted scarf around her neck and up over her chin; she stuck a wool cap on her head and worked it down as far as it would go.

Lucy felt satisfied with her disguise. She wasn't exactly sure when she'd changed her mind about the funeral, but now that she had, she felt an urgency to get the whole thing over with. She was sure no one would recognize her, and especially at a distance. She didn't plan on staying long anyway, just long enough for everyone to leave the gravesite, so she could have one last moment with Byron.

Turning abruptly, she headed for the garage. Yesterday morning she'd found Angela's car key lying on her nightstand, along with a brand-new cell phone—emergencies only—and a note from Irene encouraging her to use the Corvette. It made her uncomfortable, remembering how Irene had confiscated that same key the night Angela disappeared. There was something about using Angela's car that stirred Lucy's guilt all over again—almost as though she were *betraying* her cousin—but the truth was, she needed a car, and Irene was seldom around to offer transportation.

So as she drove slowly through the wet streets, her thoughts were focused on how ironic fate could be. The fact that she was using Angela's precious car only because Angela was missing. And the fact that she was going to the cemetery, where so many things in life ended—but where so many things in her life had begun.

The place where she'd first met Byron.

And now, the place where she would tell him good-bye.

Lucy had no trouble finding the old church that adjoined the town's even older burial grounds. By the time she arrived, the solemn cortege had wound its way along a narrow dirt lane through the graveyard and come to a respectful stop behind the hearse. Parking her car around the block where it wouldn't be noticed, she ducked her head and slipped in the back way.

The funeral was not far. The low drone of a solitary voice told her the service had already begun. To her surprise, there was a stone mausoleum instead of a grave, and like several other structures she'd noticed throughout this neglected part of the cemetery, Byron's family crypt reminded her of a miniature house for the dead. Dreary and decayed, with roof and walls draped in withered ivy, each corner was guarded by a faceless angel cradling a skull beneath its wings. Two broken urns flanked the gated doorway; the wrought-iron gates were flaked with rust. And the name WETHERLY, carved above the entrance, was nearly invisible, worn smooth by the ceaseless passing of time.

Suppressing a shiver, Lucy spotted a small grove of elm trees a safe distance behind the gathering, and hid herself deep in its shadows.

The mist had turned to light rain. Rainlike tears, wept from cold, gray sorrow. She could see the large crowd of mourners huddled together, sharing umbrellas and hugs and grief. She could hear the echo of muffled sobs. Byron might have been a loner, Lucy realized, but there was something about losing one of its own that bonded a community. Students, teachers, neighbors, strangers, old and young alike, she guessed, but especially the young people of Pine Ridge. They watched with pale, stricken faces and tragic disbelief.

Lucy shut her eyes, clamped her arms tight around her chest. A desperate wail rose up inside her and exploded in her mind, and as her eyes opened once more, she braced herself against one of the trees, not trusting her legs to hold her. She thought of Byron's grandmother, so frail and all alone. Tears streamed down her cheeks. Through the dim blur of autumn she could see Byron's coffin banked with flowers; she could see the vague figure of a priest. Words of comfort were being spoken—stories related and memories recalled—and prayers that held no meaning drifted back to her on the sad sigh of the wind.

And then it was over.

With hushed finality, people walked slowly

past Byron's casket, some adding more flowers and special mementos, some reaching out with one last touch, before wandering back to their cars. The hearse, empty now of its burden, led the procession of mourners away.

Lucy stood still for a moment as bitter reality sank in. She could see several men in work coveralls lounging across the lane, talking and laughing among buckets and tools, acting as though this were just any other ordinary day. It suddenly occurred to her that theirs was the most final job of all—that of interring Byron's coffin inside his family tomb.

With an effort, Lucy roused herself from her sorrow. She'd wanted some time alone with Byron, a private good-bye—but now she'd have to hurry before the workmen came over. Swiping a gloved hand across her cheeks, she eased from her hiding place and started toward the casket.

The feeling came without warning.

That cold prickly feeling of being watched.

Lucy froze in midstride. As her heart quickened, she turned and peered off through the drizzle, seeing nothing but headstones and crosses and statues, faint blurs beyond the rain.

Get a grip—you're imagining things.

Of course that was it, Lucy told herself firmly. Just the culmination of stress and fear, and everything else she'd endured over the past week, playing tricks with her mind.

You're just upset—not thinking straight. Hurry and do what you have to do.

Burrowing deep in her jacket, Lucy slowly approached the mausoleum. The workmen in the distance had noticed her now; she could see them shifting restlessly, anxious to finish their job, but allowing her some time. She kept her back to them and pretended they weren't there. She bent low over the coffin and ran her hands along its surface, breathing in the warm scent of the flowers, letting her sobs come at last, quiet and soul-wrenching cries of despair.

"I'm sorry, Byron," she wept. "I'm so, so sorry . . ."

She truly hadn't thought she could cry any more. But at last, empty and exhausted, she straightened up, reached into her pocket, and withdrew the heart-shaped pin. For a long moment she stared at the bouquets and personal tributes heaped upon the casket, wondering what she should do. If she left the pin on the coffin, it could so easily slide off. Become lost. Get stolen or thrown away.

She felt her eyes shifting to the family crypt.

Maybe there was another place she could put it—a hidden place no one else would ever know about. An eternal secret between Byron and her.

Squaring her shoulders, Lucy pretended to leave. She walked briskly off through the cemetery, then doubled back through the trees. From behind the mausoleum she watched the workmen gathering up their tools and strolling leisurely across the lane. She was certain they hadn't seen her—if she hurried, she'd be gone again before they even reached the tomb.

She glanced around quickly, the pin clutched tight in her glove. Beside her on a corner pedestal knelt one of the four angels, holding a ghoulish skull beneath its wings. On impulse, Lucy reached over and tried to lift the statue, surprised when it moved slightly off center. With a little effort, she managed to tip it sideways, just high enough to slide the pin under its base. Then she lowered it, gazed at where the angel's face should have been, and whispered a silent prayer.

Goose bumps crawled over her skin.

With a gasp, Lucy whirled around, her eyes probing the mist and the shadows, her heart stuck in her throat.

She was sure she hadn't imagined it this time.

Someone was watching her.

And it's someone I know . . .

Frantically she pushed the thought from her mind. It wasn't possible. She knew hardly anyone in Pine Ridge, the funeral was over, the mourners had gone, and except for the workmen she was all alone.

And yet her blood felt cold in her veins.

Because for one brief second, she could have sworn she'd seen a figure in the distance, standing still and silent among the graves.

A human figure that vanished just as soon as she'd turned to look.

5

School was even worse than before.

Lucy knew she must look like something straight from a horror movie, with her cuts and bruises and stiff, jerky movements. As she went slowly from class to class, she fought off fatigue and depression and kept her eyes averted from the other students. Since Byron's funeral she'd slept little, and even the medication Dr. Fielding had prescribed hadn't prevented the nightmares and sudden awakenings, the chills and sweats and frantic heartbeats as her mind endlessly replayed the car accident, her ordeal at the cave, her unknown rescuer, the shadowy figure at the cemetery.

After she'd returned home on Saturday she'd made up her mind not to discuss any more fears with Dr. Fielding. She knew he meant well, but she also knew he'd never believe her. Confiding in Irene was out of the question. And still being an outsider at school, there was no one Lucy could trust. If there were problems to be fixed and mysteries to be solved, it was totally up to her. She was on her own.

So she'd resigned herself to school today as Irene and Dr. Fielding had insisted, but she'd avoided any contact with her classmates. Not hard to do, Lucy thought ruefully as she made her way through the halls, all too aware of the anger and hatred aimed in her direction. She could feel the open hostility like knives in her back.

Testaments to Byron were everywhere. From the black armbands students wore, to his photographs watching her from lockers, corridors, bulletin boards, the walls of every classroom. A shrine had been set up outside the library—notes and letters, signs and posters, flowers and stuffed animals, and personal gifts. In every one of his classes, his desk remained empty, adorned with flowers and presents.

Lucy felt sick to her stomach and sick at heart. She didn't know how she was ever going to survive the day.

But besides the tributes to Byron, there were reminders of Angela, too. MISSING posters in every building, lining the halls, tucked among teddy bears, bouquets, and cards in makeshift memorials. Across the entire campus, yellow ribbons fluttered from every tree. No matter where Lucy went, she couldn't escape the guilt or the sorrow. Even the teachers seemed strangely uneasy around her, and when Principal Howser called her to his office to express sympathy and inform her she'd be meeting with a grief counselor, he kept the talk brief, as though she might be bad luck and highly contagious. By study hall, she felt like a leper.

Eager to escape, Lucy dumped her purse and books in her locker and slipped out a side door. Despite the overnight drop in temperature and the warning of possible snow, she found a bench at the far end of campus near the athletic field and sat down with her back against the fence. Irene had bought her a new coat that was fleecy and warm, and new boots perfect for winter. Lucy huddled into a snug ball and wrapped her wool scarf high around her cheeks, thrusting her mittened hands deep in her pockets. She seriously doubted she'd freeze to death out here, but even *that* prospect was more appealing than going back in to endure those accusing faces.

She let her eyes do a slow sweep of the school yard. A few kids were straggling in and out of the gym; a maintenance man on a riding mower was clearing leaves from the lawn. Several students had decided to brave the cold and were sharing notes at one of the picnic tables in the courtyard. Lucy sighed and began to tick off a mental list in her head. Her favorite purse and everything in it had been destroyed in the crash, and though she'd gotten her student ID this morning, and—thanks to Irene (who had friends in high places)—her driver's license had been reissued in no time at all, there were still some items she needed to replace. Funny how you took those little things for granted, didn't even notice them, in fact, till they were gone. Like her pen with the fuzzy top and her lucky pink stone. Chewing gum and breath mints and chocolate-covered raisins. Her mini-mirror and matching comb, the little green notepad, a tiny vial of spray perfume. Her leather key ring, with the key to her old apartment still attached.

Lucy closed her eyes and swallowed a lump in her throat.

Her red wallet and her address book, and all the pictures of the friends she'd left behind. Symbolic, somehow, she thought bitterly. Her life was different now—her *world* was different now. There was nothing and no one she could ever go back to.

She swallowed harder as tears welled behind her eyelids. Maybe it was time to fix up that bedroom she hated so much, unpack her boxes stored up in the attic, make the room her own. Maybe she should try to get a job. Buy some new clothes like Irene had been encouraging her to do. Resign herself to reality.

Reality . . . right. Being a freak and being alone.

She was so intent on her misery that she didn't even notice someone had stopped beside the bench. As she heard the sound of twigs snapping, she opened her eyes and saw a pair of raggedy sneakers planted firmly on the ground in front of her.

Lucy stared up in surprise.

"You know," the girl said somberly, "death by freezing isn't quite as painless as you might think. Even though you probably don't care much about that fact right now."

There was something vaguely familiar about this person, something Lucy couldn't quite put her finger on. So instead she returned the comment with a frown.

"I'd like to be alone, if you don't mind."

"That's probably a bad idea." The soft-spoken girl gestured toward the bench. "How about if I join you for a while?"

It was obvious she wasn't going away. Lucy considered her options, frowned harder, then grudgingly scooted over. The girl promptly sat, her legs splayed out in front of her, both arms wrapped around a beat-up knapsack. Lucy continued to frown, then felt a small stir of recognition.

"I know you. You're the girl at the Festival— the one working with Angela."

"One and the same. I'm also in homeroom and three other classes with you, but I doubt that you've noticed."

"I . . . sorry. I guess I haven't."

"Well, it's hard to notice much of anything when you're staring at your desk all the time.

And anyway, when you saw me at the Festival, I was pretty rude."

Lucy recalled her clearly now. The girl at the entrance to Pin the Nose on the Scarecrow, the one with the serious face. "You look different."

"Because I no longer have a bunch of wild brats hanging all over me." The girl gave a mock shudder. "What was I thinking anyway, volunteering for that stupid game? I don't even like kids."

Lucy's resistance melted. She could feel a hesitant smile coming on.

"Dakota." The girl held out a small, wind-chapped hand. "Dakota Montana. I swear I'm not making it up."

This time Lucy did smile. And as the two shared a handshake, she managed a quick, head-to-toe appraisal of her new acquaintance.

The girl had been frazzled and distracted at the Fall Festival, surrounded by children and distorted by colored lights—but now Lucy could see the waist-length red hair; the large, solemn, pale blue eyes; the thick straight brows; the sprinkling of tiny freckles across the fair skin of her cheekbones. Her nose was delicate; her mouth too wide for her heart-shaped face. A good three inches shorter than Lucy, she was wearing faded overalls with ripped knees, a dingy sweater that might once have been white, and the most ridiculous scarf Lucy had ever seen—at least twenty feet of it—knitted in every color of the rainbow. It was wrapped not only several times around Dakota's neck, but also draped down her chest and back, hanging all the way to her sneakers—one pink and one green—both laced with orange ribbon. Despite the unique fashion statement, there was an almost ethereal quality about her, Lucy realized—like a woodland elf or a fairy queen from some fantasy bedtime story. And as she met Dakota's eyes, the girl gave a faint smile, a smile that hinted of wisdom and experience far too old for such a young face.

"They won't act like jerks forever, you know," Dakota said quietly. "It's just because of Byron."

Lucy was taken aback. Her mouth opened, then closed again, with no words of defense. Dakota shot her a glance of sympathy, leaned back, and tucked both hands beneath the bib of her overalls.

"Everyone knows you were with him in the accident," she went on matter-of-factly. "They don't care about knowing anything else."

Lucy could barely choke out the words. "They hate me because he died and I didn't."

"Well . . ." Dakota seemed to be thinking, rocking slowly back and forth in her seat. "It's more complicated than that. They hate you because the two of you got together. And Byron never got together with anyone."

"We . . . we were just friends, if that's what you mean."

"That's *not* what I mean. And it's none of my business anyway. It's just that Byron was here for so long—in this town, in this school—and no one really *knew* him. Then *you* come to school for one day, and he actually spends time with you. You make some sort of connection with him that no one's ever made."

Lucy said nothing, only stared miserably down at her feet. *If only you knew the truth . . . if only you knew the whole story . . .*

Dakota stopped rocking, her brow creased in a puzzled frown.

"Guilt's such a weird power," she mused. "It makes people do crazy things. Mean, hateful things sometimes. And right now everyone's closing ranks, trying to figure stuff out, trying to pretend they were all Byron's friends." She paused for a moment, her voice growing hard. "Now that he's gone, they're upset and they're missing him. The school's brought in grief counselors to help them deal with it. They've put Byron's pictures all over the place. I mean . . . I didn't know Byron very well either. But I think he'd *hate* all this, all this attention from a bunch of hypocrites."

For some strange reason, Lucy felt comforted by these words. She watched as Dakota started rocking again, as the girl plucked up one end of her knitted scarf and twirled it between her fingers.

"I think you're right," Lucy said at last. "I think he *would* hate it."

Once again, Dakota went still. For a long moment the two girls stared at each other. And then they both smiled.

"You *really* didn't want to freeze to death, did you?" Dakota asked, standing up, holding out both her hands.

Still smiling, Lucy shook her head. She let Dakota pull her off the bench, then fell into step beside her as they headed back across the grounds.

"Do you know Byron's grandmother?" Lucy asked, trying not to stumble over Dakota's trailing muffler.

"I know *about* her—but no, I've never met her. To tell you the truth, I don't really know anyone who's ever been to their house."

"I heard about his sister. The rumors, I mean."

"Well," Dakota shrugged philosophically, "what does *crazy* mean anyway? I saw her around town sometimes, she and Byron—but she's been gone for quite a while. She was beautiful . . . always seemed kind of shy. And you can't believe everything you hear— especially in *this* town."

"Well . . . actually I heard it from Angela."

"Even more reason not to believe it." Dakota stopped in her tracks and looked embarrassed.

"Sorry. I shouldn't have said that. I keep forgetting you're her cousin."

"Not really. More like her stepcousin."

"Well . . . still . . ."

"We weren't that close," Lucy admitted regretfully as they started walking again.

"Hmmm. Big surprise there."

"I mean . . . *aren't* that close," she corrected herself quickly, as if speaking of Angela in the past tense would guarantee a bad ending.

Dakota threw her a knowing look. "It's okay. You're not jinxing anything by being honest."

"It's just that . . ." Lucy's voice faltered, "it's bad enough that everyone blames me for Byron. But they blame me for Angela, too."

"Not all of them, Lucy. Maybe not even *most* of them, in fact. And how could you ever think that anyway?" But at the pained expression on Lucy's face, Dakota's tone softened even more. "Oh. So I guess you *don't* know."

"Know what?"

"That this isn't the first time Angela's disappeared."

Now it was Lucy who stopped. "Wait . . . I don't understand."

"I mean she's run away from home before. *Three* times, in fact—at least that I know of. And each time there's a big search and a big investigation because her mom has a lot of clout in this community. And each time her mom hires some private detective who ends up finding Angela and bringing her back home."

Lucy felt stunned, her thoughts whirling in confusion. So was *this* all there was to the mystery? Just another of Angela's normal escapes? Another routine act of rebellion— another cry for attention? A selfish game to cause worry and fear—*and the accident—and Byron's death*—

"No," Lucy whispered, not even realizing she'd spoken aloud. *No, this time there's more to it. The mysterious stranger at the Festival . . . and the green necklace . . . and stalking shapes and bloodred moons . . .*

Every instinct had told her so then, and every instinct told her so now. This time was different. Dangerous . . . and potentially deadly.

"Deadly," she whispered again.

"What?" Dakota leaned forward, but Lucy shook her head and took a step back.

"Nothing. I just . . . nothing."

"Look, I don't mean that something bad couldn't really happen to Angela," Dakota explained, resting her hands on Lucy's shoulders. "It only takes *one* time to be the *wrong* time. And people can never be too careful." She thought a moment, then added, "But when I saw Angela at the Festival that night, it wasn't like she was being carried off against her will. She didn't act the least bit scared or upset. When she left me the envelope to give you, she seemed happier than I've ever seen her."

"So you actually saw the guy who took her away?"

"I was too busy with the kids to really notice. I saw her go off with someone, but it was from the back, and they disappeared into the crowds. The only thing I could tell the police was that he was taller than her, and he had dark hair."

Lucy shivered, remembering the deep voice, the mysterious presence, that she herself had encountered behind the scarecrow tent. "Do you think it was the same guy Angela met the night before?"

"I have absolutely no idea. Angela would flirt with anybody. I'm not surprised she'd go off with a total stranger."

"That evening before we left the house, she actually dropped some hints about running away. But I didn't catch on. It didn't hit me till later."

Dakota nodded understandingly, her hands sliding from Lucy's shoulders. The two of them picked up their pace as the bell rang for class.

"I have to help out at the bookstore tonight," Dakota told her as they approached the side entrance. "My family's bookstore, actually—Candlewick Shop. It's kind of a dumpy little place in the old part of town—but you can drink coffee there and probably find every used book in the universe. So, if you feel like company later on, why don't you come over?" She dug into one of her pockets and pulled out a card. "Here's the store number; my home number's on the back. My dad doesn't believe in cell phones. He says they're just an expensive way to annoy the people around you, and he can do that for free. Anyway, if you need a ride, just call me, and I'll come get you."

"Thanks. I just might."

They jogged the last few feet to the building. Before Dakota could reach for the door, however, it burst open, and a giggling trio of cheerleaders pushed past them. As one of them jarred Lucy's arm, Lucy immediately froze.

The girl with her friends didn't notice. She hurried with the others toward the gym, but Dakota turned and stared at the stricken expression on Lucy's pale face.

"Lucy? What is it?"

Lucy didn't answer. As she gazed after the cheerleaders, Dakota followed the direction of her shocked stare.

"Lucy?"

"That girl . . ." Lucy's voice was scarcely a breath, and Dakota moved closer to hear.

"Lucy, what's wrong?"

Lucy pointed to the girl in the middle of the threesome. "That girl . . . there . . ."

"Who? The one with the really short hair? Wanda Carver?"

"She's going to die on Thursday."

6

For a second the world went dark.

It was as though a thick black cloud had settled in Lucy's line of vision, blotting out the entire rest of the world.

And then slowly, a glimmer came through. It parted the shadows in her brain and began to glow, sending light and sensation into her body once more. With a gasp, she blinked her eyes and saw Dakota peering anxiously back at her.

"What did you just say?" Dakota murmured.

Lucy gave herself a mental shake. Her head hurt, and her legs felt as though they might crumple at any second. "I . . . I said . . ."

Sweat dripped from her forehead, though her whole body was chilled. She stared back at Dakota with a blank frown.

"I said . . ." What *had* she said? *Something about a girl . . . something about dying . . .* Lucy put a trembling hand to her temple and pressed gently.

"You're white as a sheet," Dakota informed her. "Are you going to be sick? Do you need to see the nurse?"

Lucy managed a nod. She felt Dakota take her arm and steer her through the door, and as they walked together down the hall, she tried desperately to replay what had just happened outside. *Dakota and I were talking . . . someone bumped my arm . . . and then . . .*

And then . . . what?

A vision? Yet she didn't recall actually *seeing* anything in her mind, no flashes, no pictures, only a frightening sense of . . . *of what?*

"Falling," she whispered, and Dakota tightened her hold on Lucy's arm.

"You feel like you're going to fall?" the girl asked worriedly.

And Lucy nodded again, because she didn't know what else to do, or why *falling* had swept through her brain, or what she could possibly do to understand it or stop it or make it go away—*falling . . . a rush of breathless surprise . . . a slow-motion horror of no escape . . .*

"—lie down for a while?" a nurse was asking, and in total confusion Lucy stared up at her from the edge of a cot. She could see Dakota next to her, could see the girl's lips moving, forming soundless words that Lucy could somehow hear—*"Do you want me to stay with you?"*—but the nurse said no, that Lucy would be fine, that she had specific instructions from Lucy's doctor and that Dakota should go on to class.

"I'll see you later then." Dakota's voice was normal now, as real as the concern in her eyes. "I hope you feel better, Lucy."

Lucy didn't answer. She lay on the cot and gazed at the ceiling, her body numb, her mind vacant. As though the emotions she'd experienced only minutes ago had shorted out and entirely disconnected. *Something about falling . . . something bad . . . a girl is going to fall . . . going to die . . .*

"Are you feeling any better, Lucy?" The nurse was there again, her manner efficient but kind. "I tried to call your aunt, but she's out of her office at the moment."

"You don't need to bother her. Maybe I could just lie here a few more seconds?"

"Rest as long as you'd like. Dr. Fielding has already talked with us, so don't be afraid to stop in here anytime you need to. It's very important not to rush your recovery."

Lucy watched as a curtain was drawn around her cubicle. She closed her eyes and tried to relax, but the message in her head began to filter through at last, crystal clear and knife-sharp. *"She's going to die . . . She's going to die on Thursday."*

My God, where had that *come* from?

Dakota had given her such a strange look when it happened. *Did she hear what I said?* Lucy honestly couldn't be sure—but then again, she wasn't even sure now if she'd actually spoken the words out loud. *Maybe I didn't say anything . . . or maybe I said something different, something I don't even remember.*

"Memory lapses," she reminded herself, fighting for calm. "The doctor said I might have memory lapses. He said they were perfectly normal."

But *Byron* had said things to her, too—*proved*

things to her, too; warned her about feelings and powers and circumstances she'd be helpless to control.

So what if those powers were getting stronger? What if she was starting to turn into Katherine?

Oh, Byron, I'd give anything to talk to you now.

Exhausted, Lucy took a deep breath and slowly let it out. She could hear someone coughing in the next cot. She could hear the distant rumble of the marching band as they practiced on the athletic field. And then she heard a low exchange of voices just outside the curtain to her cubicle.

"Would it be possible to see her?" someone was asking in a hushed voice, definitely male. A familiar voice, too, Lucy thought. One she'd heard before and not so long ago.

"Of course," the nurse replied. "Principal Howser told me Lucy was scheduled to meet with you this afternoon."

Lucy gave an inward groan. *Oh, great. Just what I need right now. A stupid grief counselor.*

"She's right in here," the nurse directed.

"Thanks."

Lucy thought about feigning sleep. But at the last instant her curiosity got the better of her, and she opened her eyes just as the curtain drew back. She caught a glimpse of tousled brown hair . . . black clothes . . . a priest's collar . . .

"Welcome back, Lucy," Matt said. "It's so good to see you again."

7

He'd been disappointed that she wanted to leave.

Deeply disappointed, but not at all surprised.

He had known he couldn't keep her there forever, that eventually she would wake within the shadows, that awareness would begin to rouse her senses once again.

She would realize then that things were not as they should be in her world.

And then she would find strength she never knew she had.

And she would flee from him.

Believing that she truly had escaped.

Now, every time he thought of it, the irony made him smile.

Her wild, desperate flight through the woods—and how he'd always been just one step ahead of her, one step behind her, so close that he could smell her wild, delicious fear and the blood throbbing madly through her veins.

The blood that was partly his own . . .

The blood he had given her from his own lips . . .

She'd been practically dead by the time he got her to the cave.

Cold and motionless, yet still beautiful.

He had undressed her so carefully and tended her wounds. Licking her blood away . . . loving the taste of it.

At times she had moaned, moving instinctively beneath his mouth.

And he had stood there for hours in the dark, gazing down on her, his mind filled with an eternity of possibilities and desires.

Undiluted, his own blood would have killed her. So rich and pure and ageless, that the shock of it to her system would have been more than her mortality could bear.

So he had done the next best thing.

After all, he'd had no time for hunting—not for the prey he preferred and was accustomed to. So he had contented himself with smaller game instead—rabbits and squirrels and foxes—and after feeding on them, he had mixed their blood with his own and coaxed it between her pale, pale lips. And after a while, when her heart beat stronger, only then had he sunk his teeth into her flesh, forcing himself to hold back, injecting only warmth and bloody spittle straight into her artery. A place no one would think to look, and a place she would never suspect.

Not that it mattered anyway.

His mark would vanish within twenty-four hours, just as it had for hundreds of years.

Leaving his victim oblivious and unscathed.

So Lucy would not know, of course, that he had saved her life.

A life so sad and lonely, that it longed to be filled with his blood and his passion.

Yes, he had touched her.

Tasted her, but not *taken* her.

A noble—and most uncommon—sacrifice on his part.

A sacrifice that left him wanting her all the more . . .

He had seen The One who rescued her.

He had stood by and watched as Lucy was lifted from the road and placed inside the car and driven far away.

And he could have resolved it then and there, but it was neither the time nor the place for confrontation.

Not the moment for settling old scores.

So he had merely suffered the anger building inside him, the hatred boiling in his veins— reminding himself it was inevitable, that he should have expected it to happen.

Truth be told, it might make the Game more interesting, this vying for Lucy's surrender.

A surrender that must be willing and complete.

A surrender that must be gradual . . . so gradual that even Lucy herself would never see it coming.

For hers was a soul to be nurtured.

Hers was a soul to be understood.

And right now, more than anything else, hers was a soul that yearned to be loved.

Loved . . .

A rare and somewhat disturbing challenge, but not altogether impossible.

He had managed it before in his lifetime, and he was *nothing* if not a Master at deception.

So he would give Lucy what she most wanted. And appear as the faces she would trust. And be exactly what she *needed* him to be.

Soon, Lucy.

Soon I'll be the only one who matters in your life.

He ached with anticipation.

And he remembered fondly all the countless hearts he'd ever stolen, knowing *hers* would be the most precious one of all.

But for now he'd let her keep it . . .

At least for a while.

8

"Matt," Lucy murmured. "What are you doing here?"

"I was just going to ask you the same thing." The young priest eased down onto the side of her cot. "You didn't have to do this to get out of our counseling session, you know. You could've just asked."

Lucy ignored the mild attempt at a joke. "I didn't know it was going to be you."

"I've been here all week. A lot of kids have needed to talk, to work through their feelings. To just . . ."

His voiced trailed off. He leaned slightly forward, hands clasped between his knees.

"Lucy . . ."

"So am I supposed to call you Father Matthew

today?" Lucy interrupted, needing to change the subject.

"Whatever you like. Whatever makes you feel comfortable."

Comfortable? She recalled the few brief encounters she'd had with Matt before her accident—when she'd escaped in terror from the confessional . . . when he'd found the necklace that was missing from Byron's pocket . . . and when he'd given out the information that had sent her and Byron on their wild-goose chase after Angela. He looked like a symbol of death sitting here, Lucy thought now—dressed in his official black, with his face so grave and composed. Just another reminder of doom and loss, and things that made no sense.

"So." Matt's eyes locked gently with hers. "How are you? Really?"

As much as Lucy wanted to avoid this conversation, she couldn't look away. She noticed the pale streaks of sunlight through his hair . . . those long dark lashes . . . that boyishly handsome face . . . everything just as she remembered. Yet *something* in Matt had changed, she realized suddenly. Some secret inner sadness? Some profound hidden pain? Whatever it was, it had darkened the deep, deep blue of his eyes and tempered his smile.

For a moment it caught her off balance. As though in some strange way she should be comforting *him*. Then her defenses rallied once more.

"How am I *doing*?" she echoed mockingly. "I'm here. That's about it."

"That's a beginning."

In a gesture that seemed professionally instinctive, his hand covered her own. Yet as an unexpected warmth touched the cold places inside her, Lucy pulled free from him and quickly sat up.

"Is this where I get the lecture?" she challenged.

"And what lecture is that?"

"The one about Byron being in a better place, and how God had some very perfect reason for killing him? And how I should just accept it and go on with my life?"

"I don't know that lecture," Matt replied seriously. "And I think the issue here is that *you* still have a life."

"Right. Lucky me."

"I'm glad you were the one with Byron at the end, Lucy. I'm glad you were the last beautiful thing he saw in this world, and maybe *that* was God's plan. Byron was a wonderful person."

"How would you know?" Lucy couldn't keep the sarcasm from her tone. "You met him one time. You didn't know him."

"You're right, I didn't know him personally. But I've heard what his classmates say about him; I know he had friends he wasn't even aware of. I know he was close to his family, looked out for his older sister, took care of his grandmother. I know he shouldn't have died so young."

Lucy's eyes filled. She barely managed a nod.

"But there's something else I know." Matt stared down at the floor, his voice low and calm. "I know that as hard as it is to lose people we care about, sometimes it's even worse being the ones left behind."

Silence stretched between them. When Lucy finally spoke, her words were bitter.

"How about being the one everyone blames?"

"You know better than that."

"If I hadn't come to Pine Ridge, none of this would have happened."

"But *something* would've happened, Lucy. Things *always* happen. They would've just happened in different ways. That's called *life*."

Lucy hesitated. Her voice came out a broken whisper. "But I keep thinking about his grandmother. Who's going to take care of Byron's grandmother?"

"She has a nurse who comes through the week. And Mrs. Dempsey, who cleans at the church, is staying nights with her temporarily. Just till other arrangements can be made."

"What other arrangements?"

"Right now we're trying to find family members we can contact. Byron's sister—Katherine—moved away about a year ago, and no one seems to know where."

Lucy felt her heart skip a beat. Without even realizing it, she clenched her right hand, as though she could squeeze away the tiny half-moon scar. "There *must* be other relatives."

"Father Paul and I are working on it," Matt replied, but Lucy could tell he was discouraged.

"And what if you can't find anyone else?"

"Then I don't think we'll have a choice. She'll have to be moved to some sort of long-term care."

The ache in Lucy's heart grew worse. "Have you been to see her yet? Does she actually realize what's happened?"

She watched as Matt shifted positions. He leaned toward her slightly, his expression puzzled.

"The sheriff asked Father Paul and Mrs. Wetherly's doctor to be there with him when he told her about the accident. So Father Paul and I rode over with the sheriff that night, and the doctor drove up the same time we did."

While Lucy remained quiet, Matt cleared his throat and stared past her, frowning at a spot on the wall.

"It was so strange," he finally said. "I don't know what I was expecting, really. But when we all got there, the front door was unlocked and the porch light was on. And Mrs. Wetherly was propped up in bed, almost as if she'd been waiting for us. She didn't even look surprised. Just so sad . . . calm . . . resigned, almost."

A shiver went up Lucy's spine. Byron had told her how his grandmother *knew* things—how she'd even warned him that he'd never see Katherine alive again. *Did she see something the night of the accident, too? Did she know about me? Did she already know Byron was dead?*

"I have to get to class," Lucy said suddenly.

Matt stood as she swung her legs over the side of the cot. He watched her take several deep breaths, then he reached down for her elbows, drawing her slowly to her feet. As Lucy swayed a little, Matt's arms went around her, steadying her against his chest.

"Are you sure you feel like staying at school?" His smile was uncertain. "I'd be glad to take you home instead."

Flustered, but not exactly sure why, Lucy pulled herself from his grasp. "Of course I'll stay. I'm fine."

The thought of being alone again in Irene's house was unsettling. But staying here at school, even for two more hours, made Lucy feel even worse. Opening the curtain wider, she suddenly turned to face him.

"I drove Angela's car today."

"I'll bring it over later. I'm sure I can get Mrs. Dempsey to follow me."

"But will the office let me leave with you?"

"Hey," Matt deadpanned, more like his old self, "I'm on official business for the Big Guy—they wouldn't dare mess with me."

The temptation was just too great. After a quick stop at her locker while Matt got his things from the office and checked in with Principal Howser, Lucy joined him by the main entrance and followed him to the visitors' parking lot.

"My aunt lives on Lakeshore Drive," Lucy told him as they headed through town. "Do you know where that is?"

"I do. And I think you should be very impressed with how well I've learned my way around."

She knew he was trying to keep the mood light. She wished she could join in, wished she could rid herself of the terrible burden in her heart, but neither seemed possible to her now. So instead she stared out her window, so that he couldn't see her face when she finally spoke.

"Matt . . . I'm really sorry."

His voice was genuinely surprised. "For what?"

"For the things I said. How angry I got."

"You have every right to be angry."

"I know I'm feeling sorry for myself. I know how pathetic that is . . . how self-destructive. And I know I should be thankful that I'm . . ." Her thoughts stumbled over sudden bad memories. She closed her eyes and forced herself to finish. ". . . that I got through it okay."

She opened her eyes again and bit down on her lower lip. She waited for Matt to answer, but when he didn't, she turned in the seat to look at him.

"Aren't you going to ask me?" she burst out.

Matt kept his eyes on the road. "Ask you what?"

"What everyone's probably heard about—at least heard *rumors* about. Where I was—what happened to me—after Byron's car went off the road."

"I think this is your street," Matt replied.

He turned into the exclusive neighborhood, following Lucy's directions to the house. As he pulled into the driveway, he let out a soft whistle.

"Wow. I can see why your aunt's one of All Souls' most beloved benefactors."

"Nobody loves my aunt. And don't change the subject."

"You know, a lot of our parishioners live in this neighborhood. They don't attend mass either, but I'm pretty sure their tax deductions include very generous donations to the church."

Lucy stared at him. He tapped his fingers slowly on the steering wheel, then turned off the engine. His expression was thoughtful as he faced her.

"Yes, I've heard rumors, Lucy. *And* questions. *And* lots of theories and speculations. But until I hear it straight from you, I won't believe anything. And I'd never just *assume* that you'd choose to tell me anyway."

Before she could answer, Matt was out of the car. He tapped on her window, and she opened the passenger door.

"You have a key?" he asked, and Lucy nodded. "But you don't have to come with me."

"Oh yes, I do. I always walk ladies to their doors and make sure they're safe."

In spite of herself, Lucy almost smiled. "Is that a church rule?"

"No, it's my mom's rule," he corrected her,

helping her out. "Which is even *more* sacred than a church rule. And there's no absolution when you break a mom's rule, didn't you know that? Break a mom's rule, and you suffer damnation for all eternity."

"You can walk me to the front, then—it's shorter. But you don't have to check the house. Irene just got a new security system—she swears not even a fly could get in."

The two of them went up the walkway to the wide, columned porch. Matt waited patiently while she fumbled the key into the lock, got the door open, and disengaged the alarm.

"Are you sure you're going to be okay here?" he persisted, his gaze sweeping the entry hall behind her.

"I'm sure. My aunt will be coming home . . . sometime." Then as Matt frowned, Lucy quickly added, "And a friend might be picking me up later."

"I'm glad, Lucy. You need to get out and be with people. It's okay to have some fun, you know."

Despite his good intentions, Lucy felt that familiar stab of guilt. "And here's the key to . . .

to Angela's car. It's a red Corvette. On the far side of the student lot, near the Dumpsters."

"Don't worry. I'll take care of it."

"Thanks. I really appreciate this. And I really appreciate the ride home."

"Anytime. I don't just keep office hours at school and church, you know. I'm on call twenty-four/seven."

Lucy watched him walk to his car. She watched as he backed down the driveway, and she kept on watching, long after the black Jeep had disappeared.

The wind was growing restless. Just as the weatherman had predicted, a powdery snow was beginning to fall.

She wished she'd let Matt come inside with her.

Gripping the edge of the doorway, she fought down a sudden wild urge to call him back.

You're fine. You're strong. And you're absolutely safe.

But as Lucy shut the door and locked it, she couldn't help thinking that the house felt even colder than the raw November air.

9

She hadn't planned on falling asleep.

With thoughts to sort out and homework to catch up on, taking a nap was the last thing she could afford to do.

But she'd been exhausted after Matt dropped her off. Exhausted and completely drained. So once she'd changed clothes and lain down across the bed, she'd fallen asleep so fast, she didn't even remember closing her eyes.

But the nightmares told her.

The nightmares always told her.

Nightmares like this one, that trapped her in Byron's van and in hidden caves, abandoned in the darkness and surrounded by dangers too terrible to imagine. Something was holding her down, something was making her burn, and through it all, someone in the background kept sobbing, *"She's going to die on Thursday . . . on Thursday."*

A frightened cry woke her. As Lucy lay there, groggy and disoriented, she tried to figure out where the sound had come from, then decided she must have made it herself. Bad enough to suffer the nightmares . . . even worse when they encroached upon reality.

She wasn't even sure what reality *was* anymore.

Her mind drifted back to school. To the girl coming out of the building, to the image of someone falling. Was she meant to give Wanda Carver a warning? How could she possibly approach a complete stranger like that? Offer some dire prediction that might be nothing more than the result of a head injury?

Just thinking about the consequences made Lucy shudder. Popular cheerleader Wanda Carver would tell the entire school. As low as Lucy's status already was, this bit of gossip would annihilate it completely.

Feeling depressed and defeated, Lucy sat up in bed. Why even bother telling anyone *anything*? She'd *tried* to tell people about the cave. About her escape through the woods, about the unknown stranger who'd rescued her. She knew how much people doubted her; even worse, she'd started doubting herself. She knew she couldn't prove anything about her terrifying experience, but that didn't make it less real. As real as these stitches on her head, these bruises fading from her face, the cuts and scratches healing along her arms and legs.

As real as seeing things without warning . . . as real as knowing things I can't explain.

Somewhere along the way, the fragile boundaries between Real and Unreal had shifted. Somewhere along the way, the boundaries between Seen and Unseen had begun to unravel and disappear.

Frowning, Lucy reached over to the nightstand. *That's funny . . . I could have sworn that lamp was on.*

In fact, she distinctly remembered turning it on when she'd come in earlier, right before she'd changed clothes. And she'd been staring at the lampshade, too, right after she'd stretched out on the bed.

She jiggled the switch back and forth. But when no light came on, she swore under her breath and fiddled with the lightbulb. Still no luck.

She realized then that dusk had fallen. She could see snow outside the sliding glass doors, drifting onto the little balcony. The house was very quiet. A vast, empty quiet that told Lucy she was still alone. Nervously she got up, closed the curtains, and went out into the hall, rubbing her arms against the chill. The house felt even colder now than it had that afternoon.

The light in the hall didn't work either. As Lucy felt her way to the top of the stairs, she could see only darkness below. Irene had had automatic timers installed in every room—the whole first floor should be glowing with lamps by now.

Wonderful. The electricity must be off.

Lucy stood on the landing, trying to think. It wasn't the first time the house had lost power, but it usually happened only during storms. Maybe it was something simple, like a fuse in the circuit breaker. Maybe that's why the house felt so cold.

Cautiously she reached out to grip the bannister. She'd have to go down and check the fuse box. She'd have to go all the way down to the basement. Anger flared inside her, mixed with fear. Why did Irene always have to work so late? Why couldn't she stay home and care even a little bit about Lucy's feelings?

I need a flashlight. I need to find a flashlight before I do anything else.

Lucy forced her thoughts into a more positive direction. No need to panic. She'd reset the security system after Matt left; she was completely safe. Not even a fly could get in; isn't that what Irene had promised her? Everything was fine. Everything was normal. She'd fix the circuit breaker, and then she'd turn on every single light in the house.

Taking a deep breath, she turned and headed for her bedroom. There was a flashlight in her nightstand drawer, one Irene had insisted she keep there for emergencies. In fact, Irene had flashlights stored all over the house, if Lucy could only remember now where they were. She could always call 911 if she got really scared. *Quit being such a wimp—it's not like this is any big deal.*

Yet Lucy's heart was pounding as she groped her way back along the corridor. And this time, her hand just happened to touch the door of Angela's room.

It was like receiving a shock.

The wooden panel was so icy cold that Lucy gasped and jumped back, pressing her hand to her chest.

For a second all she could do was stand there in the dark. The chill in her fingers shot all the way up through her arm, all the way into her head. She was too stunned to move; it was too black to see. Yet her eyes stared straight ahead, straight at Angela's door.

Irene had kept it shut ever since Angela's disappearance.

As though Angela and everything about her must be sealed away from Irene's disapproval and the constant demands of Irene's busy life.

Holding her breath, Lucy reached out for the door.

And felt it move slowly inward.

Angela's window was open. Lucy could see it from where she stood on the threshold, though the room was thick with shadows. The curtains fluttered like restless ghosts, and snow had swirled in through the screen, lying still unmelted upon the carpet.

Oh my God . . . someone's broken in!

Yet through a surge of panic, Lucy could see that the screen hadn't been cut, the glass was still intact.

It didn't make sense. She couldn't imagine that Irene had come in here and opened that window. And Florence came to clean only on Fridays. But maybe Florence had done it—opened the window to air out Angela's room and then forgotten to close it again. *Yes, that's it*, Lucy told herself firmly. *That must be it—what else could it be?*

But as rationalizations swept through her mind, she began to be aware of something else. It came through to her slowly and faintly, and it took her several moments even to realize what it was.

A sound. A soft, muffled sound . . . like . . . ringing?

Lucy couldn't move. With mounting fear, she strained to listen, and her brain struggled to compute. *Yes . . . definitely a ringing sound . . .*

A telephone.

Goose bumps crept along her spine. Angela's telephone was ringing, and as Lucy turned reluctantly toward the sound, she heard Angela's answering machine kick on. "Hi," purred the sultry voice. "This is Angela. If you think you can handle me, leave a message."

Nobody spoke.

Lucy heard only silence on the other end of the line.

Terrible, frightening silence . . . as someone waited.

Wrong number, Lucy thought frantically— *everyone knows Angela's missing—no one who knows her would be doing this!*

Yet she felt herself walking toward the phone. Maneuvering through the darkness, as the silence on the answering machine stretched on and on and on . . .

In slow motion, Lucy picked up the receiver.

"Hello?" she whispered.

And the voice that answered turned her blood to ice.

"It's so dark here," Angela sobbed, "I can't get back!"

"*Angela!*" Lucy screamed.

She pressed the receiver hard against her ear, her voice rising in panic, her heart racing out of control.

"Angela! It's Lucy! Where are you? Are you okay?"

But there was nothing but static now.

"*Angela!*"

Frantically, Lucy began pushing buttons, but there was no voice, no dial tone, and after several more seconds, no noise at all.

"Hello?" she cried. "Hello? *Angela!* Angela, don't hang up—please talk to me!"

In desperation Lucy jerked the telephone from Angela's desk.

And that's when the truth finally hit her.

The cord was plugged into the wall.

But the electricity was still out.

10

It's a trick—it has to be some kind of trick!

Dropping everything, Lucy ran into the hallway and stumbled the last few feet to her room.

A cruel, sick joke! Kids from school tormenting me, because of Byron, because of Angela—

She locked her door and braced her back against it. Blood pounded in her ears, and her body jolted with every terrified heartbeat.

"Guilt's such a weird power . . . It makes people do crazy things . . . Mean, hateful things sometimes . . ."

Hadn't Dakota tried to warn her? Hadn't Dakota tried to warn her just today?

Lucy's head spun wildly. Maybe Dakota wasn't really who she seemed to be; maybe she wasn't a friend at all. Maybe her warning had all been part of this huge, sick joke she and her *real* friends had already been planning to spring on Lucy . . .

Calm down. Breathe. Think.

Lucy's palms pressed flat against the door. Her spine was rigid. Her vision blurred, then focused. Her eyes made a slow, thorough sweep of the shadows. The sliding glass doors were still shut; no invisible presence alerted her instincts to danger. Long minutes crept by. Finally she forced herself over to the nightstand and took the flashlight from the drawer.

The bright beam of light was a lifeline.

Still shaking, Lucy went into the bathroom and locked the connecting door to Angela's room. Then she sat down on the edge of her bed and gripped the flashlight to her chest.

Damn them! How could anyone be so mean, so heartless? Hadn't she been through enough? Would guilt and blame cling to her for the rest of her life?

Yet she couldn't figure out how they'd done it, how they'd managed to rig the whole scenario. Even with high-tech knowledge, wouldn't someone have had to get into the house to pull it off? Maybe they'd caused the power outage, too. But how had they managed to bypass such a sophisticated security system? It just didn't make any sense.

Unless . . .

Lucy's breath caught in her throat. She squeezed the flashlight tighter, so tight that her fingers ached.

No! No, what happened back there in Angela's room *couldn't* have had anything to do with psychic powers or gifts or curses. Her body hadn't signaled her like it so often had in the past. She hadn't seen visions; there hadn't been a feeling or impression or a warning too overwhelming to ignore. What had happened just now wasn't like anything she'd ever experienced. *So, no. No! It couldn't have been just me.*

Yet no matter how much she argued with herself, she couldn't quite shut out the whisper in her mind. The persistent little whisper that kept nagging her, trying to get through. *What if it's not a joke? What if it's real? What are you going to do?*

Moaning softly, Lucy lowered her head and cradled it in her arms. *No, no, there's a logical explanation, it's a horrible trick, and Florence just forgot and left the window open!* Because she couldn't bear to think otherwise. Because the sound of Angela's voice and the prospects of Angela's fate were just too chilling to imagine.

Imagine? Maybe I did imagine it. Maybe I had a memory lapse or blacked out or hallucinated. One of those things that people with head injuries are supposed to do.

Helplessness engulfed her. She couldn't call the police—they'd never believe her. She couldn't tell Irene—her aunt would put her straight into the hospital. So who? Dr. Fielding with his comfort-coated skepticism? All Lucy knew for sure was that she couldn't stay here a minute longer. She had to leave, and she had to leave *now*.

Leading with the flashlight, she hurried downstairs, yanked her coat from the closet, and stopped to check the battery backup on the security system.

And that's when she remembered she didn't have a car.

What time is it anyway?

She looked at her watch, surprised to see that

it was after seven. Surely Matt should have been here by now—surely he would have rung the doorbell when he dropped off the car.

Lucy pulled aside the front curtains and peered out at the driveway. The red Corvette was sitting there, parked about halfway down, covered with a thin layer of snow.

That's strange . . .

Grabbing her purse, she slammed the door behind her. But as she cut across the lawn and got closer to the car, she began to slow down.

The last thing in the world she wanted to do right now was drive that thing. Not after what had just happened upstairs. Not after what she'd just heard.

Lucy stopped. She stared at the Corvette and felt tiny prickles of apprehension creep along her spine. Maybe she should call a cab. She had no clue about taxi service here in Pine Ridge— *or* the drivers. And right now she didn't trust anybody. *Not anybody. Not even myself.*

She took her time going around the sports car, brushing off the feathery snow, shining her flashlight in all the windows. She told herself she was being silly; she told herself she was being safe. When she tried the handle, the door came open, unnerving her even more.

Why didn't Matt lock it? Why didn't he at least tell me he was here?

Climbing inside, she noticed the air was slightly warm, as though the heater had only recently been shut off. She closed the door and began hunting for the key.

Both visors were empty. Lucy ran her hands along the floor mats, then rummaged nervously through the glove box. She searched the backseat area but found nothing. Maybe it wasn't here at all. Maybe Matt had forgotten to leave it. Leaning her forehead on the steering wheel, she tried to stay calm. Snow was thickening on the windshield, and the car was getting cold.

On a whim, Lucy bent down and began groping beneath the seats. Far back under the driver's side, her fingers made contact with something soft and bulky, like thick cloth. It had been wedged in so tight, it took several minutes of intense pulling to finally work it free.

Lucy stared down at the bundle in her hands.

By the glow of her flashlight, she began to open the heavy folds of fabric. A blanket of some kind . . . a blanket that seemed familiar . . . covered with dead leaves and pine needles and stained with mud . . .

And with something wrapped inside it . . .

"No," Lucy whispered. "Oh God . . ."

Most of the jacket was burned away—just charred holes and black tatters—yet Lucy recognized it at once. Remembered the way it had looked on Byron the very first time she'd met him . . . and in that last split second before the crash.

She needed air. She couldn't breathe. The car was too small, too suffocating, and she clawed at the door, but it wouldn't open.

She didn't even notice the car key as it fell out of the blanket. Or when it landed on the floor at her feet.

She only saw the snowflakes turning to ashes as she slumped forward over the steering wheel.

11

"Lucy," the voice was saying. "I've got you, Lucy—you're safe."

Someone was holding her.

She could feel strong arms around her, and her head was tilted sideways, resting on somebody's chest.

"Let's get you inside," the voice murmured.

I know that voice.

"Lucy? Just relax . . . just lean against me."

Yes . . . yes . . . I know that voice, but I can't quite place it . . .

For a split second of panic, Lucy thought she might be back again, back in the places of her nightmares, back in the shadowy cave, the cold wet woods, the deserted road. But then, as her eyes began to open, she could see a world of pure white, and a door with a large brass knocker that looked vaguely familiar.

"Nobody's answering," the voice was telling her now. "Where the hell's your aunt?"

Lucy barely managed to shake her head.

"Then what's the code?" the voice asked. "Lucy, can you give me the code?"

The code . . .

Weakly, she squinted up into a face. A worried face, but calmly reassuring as well. His hair was sifted with snowflakes, and as a gust of wind hit the two of them, he drew Lucy closer into his warmth.

"Matt?" she whispered.

"Do you remember the security code, Lucy?" he asked her again. "I need to get you inside."

Her head was beginning to clear. She realized they were on the front porch, and that she was shivering from head to toe. With sudden clarity, images of the blanket and burned jacket burst into her mind, and she immediately began to struggle.

"Hey, calm down," Matt held her tighter. "I told you, everything's okay—"

"No, those things in the car!"

"What things?"

"In the car—the blanket, Byron's jacket— you must have seen them—"

"Lucy, I didn't see anything but you. What are you talking about?"

"He put them there! He must know where I live—how can he *know* that?"

"Ssh . . . Listen to me—"

"Why did you leave the car unlocked? Why didn't you make sure no one was following you? You must have led him straight here!"

"Stop it, Lucy, you're not making any sense." The shake he gave her was gentle, but firm. "Whatever this is about, we'll *discuss* it. I *promise*. But right now we need to go inside without setting off the alarm and looking like two half-wit burglars."

"But I *want* the police to come! They need to get fingerprints and DNA—"

"Lucy. Tell me the code."

The tone of his voice got through to her at last. It took her several minutes, but she was finally able to recite the correct numbers in their proper sequence. Then Matt turned the key, stepped into the house, and—following

Lucy's garbled directions—disarmed the system.

"Where's the couch?" Pausing at the foot of the stairs, he raised a quizzical eyebrow and looked for a place to set her down. "Couch, chair, or bed. Your choice."

But Lucy was babbling again. "The blanket? It was the one I took when I was trying to escape. The police will *have* to believe me now."

"Where would you be the most comfortable?"

"No, no, I can walk."

"Don't argue with me."

Seeing the determination on his face, Lucy pointed to a doorway. "The den's through there. But you've *got* to call the police, Matt. He had Byron's jacket, don't you understand? The same one Byron was wearing when we crashed! How could he have Byron's jacket? And I lost that blanket in the woods, so how did he find it? Why is he doing this to me?"

"Hush, Lucy." Carefully Matt lowered her to the couch, then began unbuttoning her coat. "Take this off and wrap up in something warm." He pulled the wool afghan from one end of the sofa and tucked it snugly around her. "I should probably take you to the emergency room. You're half frozen."

"Don't call a doctor—call the *police*! Haven't you heard a single word I've said?"

"What about tea? Do you like tea?"

Frustrated, Lucy grabbed his sleeve. "Listen to me. You've *got* to get that stuff from the car. I didn't have any evidence before, but now I do, and if he's out there right now watching us, the police might be able to catch him!"

"If *who's* out there watching us?" Matt demanded, easing himself from her grip. But as Lucy grew more agitated, he knelt down in front of her and took both her hands in his. "Yes, okay, I'll go out to the car. And if it's necessary, I promise I'll call the police. But first I'm going to fix you something hot to drink so we can get your blood flowing again."

"You're wasting time!"

"Time? Well, speaking of time, just how long were you lying out there unconscious in the car?"

"I don't know. What time is it now?"

Matt glanced at the clock on the fireplace

mantel, then double-checked his watch. "Your clock's wrong. Mine says about eight-thirty."

"That can't be right." Lucy stared at him in amazement. "I couldn't have been out there for nearly an hour."

"An hour? People have frozen to death in *half* that time!"

"It wasn't *that* cold. In fact, the car was still warm inside."

Now it was Matt's turn to look surprised. "That's impossible. I brought it over about five o'clock."

"But I'm sure it was . . ." Her voice trailed off as something began to dawn on her. "Matt, the electricity's on."

For the first time since they'd come in, she noticed the glare of the foyer light, the glow from surrounding lamps, the stuffy heat and muted hum of the furnace. Matt was staring at her as if she might clarify her remark with some earth-shattering revelation.

"It wasn't on before," she murmured.

"So that explains why your clock's wrong."

"Someone *shut* it off."

His expression grew more puzzled. "Shut your *clock* off?"

Before he could question her further, Lucy threw the afghan aside and stood up, only to feel Matt's hands on her shoulders, pushing her down again.

"Where do you think you're going?"

"To the car. I'm telling you, someone shut off the electricity in this house tonight. And someone deliberately put stuff in the car. And if you're not going to help me, then I'll do it myself."

"Okay, okay. Hold on." Sighing in defeat, Matt turned toward the hall. "I'll go."

"A blanket. And a jacket. They're both in the front seat."

"Right. But in the meantime, I want you to stay here and cover up again."

Lucy did as she was told. She sat huddled beneath the afghan, her mind spinning in a dozen different directions. Questions pounded at her brain. She could feel her body beginning to thaw, but fears and suspicions sent a different kind of chill to her heart.

She heard a door slam and looked up to see

Matt poised in the threshold. He was holding the car key in his hand.

The car key and nothing else.

"Where are they?" Lucy's voice rose hopefully. "You found them, didn't you? In the front, like I said?"

But when Matt didn't answer, the chill deepened inside her.

"No," Lucy whispered.

She saw him hesitate . . . saw the concern and sympathy in his eyes.

"Lucy—" he began, but she cut him off with an angry shout.

"*No!* Those things were *there*! I didn't imagine them—I'm *not* crazy!"

"Of course you're not crazy." Matt spread his hands in a conciliatory gesture. "I don't think that, Lucy. Nobody thinks that—"

"*Everybody* thinks that!"

"You're wrong. Please don't get upset. Just tell me what's going—"

"Maybe he did it at school! He could have broken in, right? In the student parking lot, when no one was looking? Can you tell if anybody broke in?"

"Who are you talking about? Nobody broke into your car at school—"

"How can you be sure? Did you check?"

"Lucy—"

"Then why did you just leave the car out there in the driveway where anyone could get in? Why didn't you come to the door and tell me you were here?"

"I *did* go to the door. I rang the bell over and over, but nobody answered. You said you might be with a friend tonight. I figured you'd gone out."

Was he telling the truth? Maybe the power outage had affected the doorbell. Had she been asleep?

"And I tried to call, too," Matt went on, "but nobody ever picked up. So I decided to drive by again, just to see if you'd gotten home." When Lucy didn't comment, he took a step toward her. "What's going on, Lucy? What's this all about?"

Lucy kept silent. She *wasn't* delusional! She could still see the scorched remains of Byron's jacket; she could still see the blanket with its crumbled, dead leaves. She'd *used* that blanket—she'd *touched* that jacket. No delusion could ever be that real!

"I'll get them myself," she muttered.

Before he could answer, she marched determinedly toward the hall. But halfway across the room, as a thought suddenly hit her, Lucy stopped and turned back to face him.

"Where was the key?" she asked.

Matt's frown was puzzled. "On the floor of the driver's seat."

"No," Lucy corrected. "I mean, where did you leave it when you brought the car over?"

He didn't even hesitate. "On the front porch. Under the mat."

12

It was strange, he thought, how a person's possessions could still retain such a part of them after death.

Like Angela's car, for instance.

It still smelled of her, even now. A smell so ripe and reckless, he could have found it anywhere in the world without any effort at all.

Expensive perfume . . . cigarette smoke . . . strawberry lip gloss and nail polish. Sex and desperation. Longing and sheer bad luck.

Smells that wafted so strong on the wind, even the snow couldn't dull them.

Sometimes he could still taste her eagerness.

But those memories were becoming more and more of an irritation to him. Taunting him when he yearned to be filled. Tormenting him when he ached to be satisfied.

Perhaps he shouldn't have been so hasty.

Perhaps he should have kept her longer . . . drawn out the deception more slowly . . . built the suspense to a more shocking and shattering climax.

At least . . . until Lucy was his.

His and his alone.

Ah, Lucy . . .

She was rarely out of his sight anymore . . . *never* out of his thoughts.

And she so innocently, so sweetly, unaware.

Believing him to be merely an errant breeze, blowing cold across her cheek.

Or the subtle stirring of a shadow coupling with her own.

Or the deep, impenetrable night gazing back at her beyond her sliding glass doors.

How could she know that *he* was the reason for her emptiness? The longing and restlessness she couldn't seem to absolve or understand?

So making use of Angela's car tonight had been gratifying to him in many ways.

Reminding Lucy of their special bond. Their past together that she so wished to forget . . .

their inevitable future she could not yet begin to imagine.

And dispelling those last lingering scents of Angela, once and for all. The car belonged to Lucy now, and it should *smell* like Lucy.

And there was no smell stronger than fear.

He preferred to think of it as a sort of exorcism.

One more move in his Game.

The Game Lucy would never win, no matter how many clues she might unravel, no matter how far ahead she believed herself to be.

The Game with Lucy as his prize.

But that wouldn't happen for a while yet.

Not when the mere *playing* of the Game was so much fun.

Especially when one played without rules.

13

"How could that key have ended up in the car if I didn't even know where it was?" Lucy's eyes were wide and fearful. "Doesn't that prove *anything* to you?"

"Lucy—"

"How did he find me, Matt? Why is he doing this?"

But before Matt could answer, Lucy pushed past him and ran outside.

"Lucy, wait!"

She was already halfway across the lawn. Even though she knew in her heart it was useless; even though she knew that when she looked inside the car, there would be no evidence whatsoever of her ordeal in the cave, not a single trace of Byron's untimely death.

Lucy yanked open the door. Her eyes made a

desperate sweep of the empty front seat, the empty floor. With a choked cry, she fell inside and started rummaging beneath the seats. Then she popped the latch and stumbled around to the trunk, lifting the cover, staring stupidly into one more empty space.

She should have known. Of course she should have.

"It's a trick," she mumbled. She wasn't even aware of Matt standing there now, reaching for her shoulder, trying to pull her away. "A trick," she kept mumbling. "A trick . . . a trick . . . how could anyone be so mean . . ."

"Come back to the house," Matt urged quietly. "Come back and get warm."

"But it couldn't be a trick, could it? No one else would know these things . . . no one else would have these things . . . so it must be real . . . somehow . . . it must be real—"

"Come on, Lucy. Please."

Lucy stepped back from the car. Through misty eyes she watched Matt close the trunk and slip out of his jacket. He threw it around her shoulders and led her back inside.

"Is the kitchen this way?" he asked her.

She wasn't even sure if she nodded. Every inch of her—body, mind, soul—had gone numb. She tried to think of Byron. Tried to remember all the things he'd told her, all the things he'd warned her about. Things about Katherine . . . powers and visions . . . the green necklace. Things about death and evil, and being stalked. Things about her life never being the same . . .

"I'm not crazy," Lucy whispered.

She realized they were in the kitchen now, that she was being pushed into a chair. Had the light been on in here before? She couldn't remember. Had the person who'd been in the car also been in the house tonight? Turning off the electricity, creeping through the halls? Leaving his mark on Angela's answering machine . . . watching Lucy while she slept?

"I'm . . . not . . . crazy."

But she felt like she was drowning. In a bottomless sea of darkness. Beneath crushing waves of despair. As though the entire world had gone black and swallowed her alive.

"Lucy," Matt said softly.

When had he crouched down beside her?

When had he eased his coat from her shoulders and draped it over the back of her chair? And when had he taken both her hands between his, rubbing them gently, trying to warm them? She could see his lips moving ever so slightly. Speaking silent words, with his head bowed and his hair windblown in long thick strands across his forehead.

"What do you do," Lucy murmured, "when nothing in your life makes sense anymore?"

Matt made a perfunctory sign of the cross. Then his eyes lifted calmly and settled on hers.

"Why don't you tell me what's wrong."

"And I don't mean just *make sense*," Lucy went on, as if he hadn't spoken. "It's more than that. Things that can't be explained. Things that are so bizarre and so unbelievable, they actually *defy* reality. Except they *are* real. They *are* happening. And there you are. You're . . . you're just *trapped* there, in the middle of it. With no one who can understand. With no one who could possibly help."

Matt's gaze never wavered. "I'm not here to push you, Lucy. And the last thing I'd *ever* want to do is interfere where I'm not wanted. But I *would* like to help you. Whatever this is, you don't have to face it alone."

"You can't," Lucy whispered even lower than before.

"Why not?"

"You just can't help me."

"Then if *I* can't, I'll find someone who *can*. But you've got to tell me what's wrong."

I have powers, she longed to tell him. *And my world isn't like everyone else's, and nothing will ever be the same again, and I'm not even sure what's real anymore, I'm afraid I'm losing my mind.*

But instead she told him, "Even if I could . . . you wouldn't understand."

"Try me. You might be surprised."

"I don't want any more surprises tonight."

Matt hesitated, seemed to consider a moment, then slowly released her hands. "Where's the tea?" he asked.

"The thing is," Lucy went on, oblivious, "if I could only have taken those things to the police, maybe then they would have taken me seriously. But I can't tell them about it now. If I do, I'll look less credible than ever."

"Am I close?" Matt was rummaging his way

through every door and drawer in the kitchen. "Am I in the general vicinity? Can you at least give me a clue?"

"Sometimes, when things like this happen, then I start thinking maybe they're right. The police and the doctors and even my aunt . . . then I start thinking maybe I really *am* crazy."

"You're not crazy."

"How do you know?"

"Ah!" Matt sounded pleased with himself. "Orange spice tea. Smells good, too. Now, let's see . . . cups."

"But I know what I saw in the car. I didn't imagine what I saw."

"I'll just zap these in the microwave."

"It couldn't have been a flashback, could it? I mean . . . Dr. Fielding said things can come back to you when you've gone through a trauma."

"Done," Matt announced. "Sugar? Lemon? Cream?"

"Sugar and lemon."

"Ah, a woman after my own heart."

Another patient exploration, this time through canisters, the refrigerator, the silverware drawer. Finally Matt set her hot tea in front of her—

complete with spoon, sliced lemon, and sugar bowl—and took a seat directly across the table.

The silence went on for minutes. Lucy stared morosely at her steaming cup.

"If you can't tell me everything," Matt suggested at last, "then tell me what happened with the car tonight. At least just that."

After another lengthy pause, Lucy nodded. Slowly stirring her tea, she related the whole incident to him without once looking up. When she was finished, silence fell between them again.

"You don't believe me," she finally whispered.

Frowning slightly, Matt leaned toward her across the table. "I didn't say that. The thing is . . . why would someone have Byron's jacket? You said Byron was wearing it when you crashed, so it was obviously . . . destroyed."

Lucy winced at the thought, and his expression softened.

"And even if it hadn't been, I can't imagine anyone taking it from the scene of the accident. There were only emergency people there, right? Police, firemen, paramedics?"

Lucy gave a reluctant nod. She knew Matt

was right—it was next to impossible that Byron's jacket could have survived the fire in any way, shape, or form.

"And what about this blanket?" Matt persisted.

Lucy paused, frowning. She hadn't told Matt any details of her horrific ordeal; she'd kept her account to the barest minimum. For just an instant she actually considered confiding everything to him. But then, taking a deep breath, she opted to keep quiet. And tell a white lie.

"The heater was broken in Byron's van so he gave me a blanket to keep warm. When I woke up after the accident, I didn't know where I was, and I tried to find help. And then I lost the blanket when I was running."

"Oh. I see."

Lucy's heart fluttered. Matt's face was carefully composed, but she had an uneasy feeling that he hadn't believed a word of her story.

"So what was all that panic about earlier?" Matt asked her now. "You wanting the police to find fingerprints and DNA?"

Lucy hedged. "Is that what I said?"

He continued to watch her. Lucy quickly took a sip of her tea, relieved when he let the subject drop.

"So who knew about the blanket?" he asked instead.

"The police. The doctors. Irene, of course."

"Well, there you go," Matt said reasonably. "You've got to remember, Pine Ridge is a small town. From what I've been told—and am *definitely* starting to witness firsthand—*everyone* eventually ends up knowing everyone else's business."

Lounging back, he rested one foot on his opposite knee, and settled himself more comfortably in his chair. He didn't look at all like a priest tonight, Lucy noted, not in his faded jeans and flannel shirt and scuffed hiking boots. She waited while he placed both hands around his cup and stared down into the steam, his expression thoughtful.

"Dozens of people could've talked about that blanket—or overheard someone else talking about it."

Lucy pondered this. "So . . . what are you getting at?"

"Have you ever considered that someone's just trying to scare you?" Matt asked. "Deliberately upset you? Just plain mess around with your head?"

Guilt's such a weird power . . . It makes people do crazy things . . . Mean, hateful things sometimes . . .

Once again, Dakota's warning came back to her. As Lucy listened to Matt repeating the very same theory, she didn't know whether to laugh or cry.

"Kids at school?" she managed at last. "Is that what you mean?"

"Well . . . I just know how cruel kids can be. Especially at an overly emotional time like this."

Lucy wanted to believe him—wanted *so much* to believe him. It made perfect sense that anyone in town could have overheard specific details of her post-accident experience. And of course it was entirely possible—and probable—that some of those who blamed her for Byron's death could have staged something simply to frighten her.

"But why the car?" she asked. "And why tonight?"

Matt shrugged. "Convenience? Maybe they've

been waiting for a chance, and opportunity finally presented itself. Everybody knows Angela's car—and it was the only one in the parking lot this afternoon. Maybe they tried to break in then, but couldn't. Anyone could've followed me here. Watched where I put the key. Planted the blanket and jacket, then taken them out again after you went inside."

"But it *was* Byron's jacket. It *was* the same blanket."

"Lucy, you had a flashlight and that little dome light in the top of the car. There's no way you could've seen anything clearly. And you panicked. And I'm sure whoever did this was counting on exactly that."

Should she tell him about the telephone call, too? About the terrified voice—*Angela's voice*—that couldn't possibly have come through during the power outage? While Matt continued his speculations, Lucy debated what to do. She opened her mouth, then shut it again, and realized she was afraid. Afraid of the answer. Afraid she'd only imagined it. And even more afraid that she hadn't.

"Lucy?"

Matt's voice pulled her back again. Taking another sip of tea, Lucy tried to focus.

"Look," Matt was explaining, "I'm not saying that any of those kids really did anything. I'm just saying they *could* have. You're in a very fragile state right now, and the worst thing you could do is jump to conclusions."

Lucy squeezed more lemon into her cup. *No, I have to bring it up*, she decided. *I have to ask him.*

"Do you think—" she began, but Matt had stood up and pushed back his chair, the scraping sound on the hardwood floor drowning out her attempted question.

"When will your aunt be home?" he asked, rinsing out his cup in the sink.

"I don't know. She works a lot."

"So you're here by yourself most of the time?"

She nodded, though his back was still to her.

"Well, you may be by yourself, but you're never alone."

His reply startled her, caught her off guard. "What do you mean?"

Matt turned around, drying his hands on a dish towel. A faint smile touched his lips. "What do you think I mean? You always have the power with you."

Lucy's heart skipped a beat. *Power?* No one knew about her power—*only Katherine, only Byron—nobody else—how could Matt possibly—*

"His power's always with you," Matt said, tossing aside the dish towel, leaning against the counter, folding his arms casually across his chest.

"Oh." Lucy could hardly swallow. "You mean God."

Matt shrugged, still smiling that faint smile.

"To tell you the truth, I don't think God's been around for a while." The bitter words were out before she could stop them. She saw Matt raise an eyebrow, and she added quickly, "If God were here, He'd make things better, right? If God were here, He'd . . . He'd make things not hurt so much."

Matt lifted one hand, thoughtfully stroked his chin. "Yeah," he finally told her. "Hurting really sucks."

They stared at each other for several long moments. In spite of herself, Lucy almost smiled. "Did they teach you that at priest school?"

"Actually, I figured it out all on my own."

Grinning, Matt picked up his jacket and walked over. He reached out and playfully ruffled her hair.

"I've got church stuff to do, Lucy. But I don't feel right about leaving you just now."

"It's okay," she assured him. "I'm fine."

As Matt looked deep into her eyes, she could read the reluctance in his own. He seemed to be waging a fierce battle with his conscience.

"Go," Lucy insisted. "Irene's bound to be home before too much longer. And I'll lock up the minute you're out the door."

"Swear?"

"Swear."

But deep down Lucy wished he wouldn't go. She *wasn't* fine, and she was afraid to be alone after all that had happened tonight.

She told Matt good-bye at the door. She watched from the window as he got in his Jeep and drove away. Then, telling herself not to be such a coward, Lucy marched upstairs and went straight to Angela's bedroom.

Matt's right. I couldn't see clearly in the car.

She turned on all the lights. She closed the window and locked it.

Everything Matt said makes perfect sense.

She forced herself to take the telephone from the desk. She lifted the receiver and listened to the dial tone. She checked for messages, but there were none at all.

But I answered the phone, so of course the call wouldn't have recorded anyway.

Lucy replaced the receiver and stepped back.

The room was still cold, neat as a pin, everything organized and perfectly in place. *Not like Angela's room at all.*

And it struck Lucy then. How vacant it felt in here, despite all the furniture. How impersonal and abandoned.

Like an empty shell.

Or a body without a soul.

As if Angela would never come back to it again.

14

"She told you to take a cab home?" Dakota was clearly puzzled. "No one ever takes cabs in Pine Ridge, except for really old people. And we only have two cabs."

Wincing slightly, Lucy shifted her backpack to her other shoulder. "She said she couldn't leave work to pick me up. And I think she was upset that I asked her to drive me this morning. But the thing is, I've never driven in snow before."

"Two inches? Believe me, this is nothing—it's already starting to melt. You haven't even *begun* to see snow yet. Just wait a few weeks."

"Does it snow a lot here?"

"Not nearly as much as I'd like it to. And it's not that hard to drive in. They're pretty good about keeping the streets plowed, and I could help you practice. And till you feel more confident, you can just ride with me when it snows."

"That's really nice of you. Thanks."

Dakota watched closely as Lucy drank from the water fountain. "You still seem a little unsteady. Are you sure you should even be here today?"

"Doctor's orders." Lucy gave a wan smile. "And Irene's. Anyway, I'm behind enough in my classes as it is."

"If you don't mind coming to the bookstore, we could study together."

Before Lucy could answer, the first bell rang. There was an immediate chorus of voices yelling, locker doors slamming, and feet pounding up and down the nearby stairs.

"I meant to stop by last night." Lucy tried to speak over the commotion. "But I fell asleep. I guess I was more tired than I thought."

"Well, after what you've been through, who wouldn't be?"

The two of them started down the hall, shouldering bravely through a surge of fellow students. Lucy tried to convince herself that no one was pointing or staring at her today, but her senses told her otherwise.

"What exactly are people saying I've been through?" she asked Dakota cautiously.

Dakota shrugged. The knitted cap she was wearing this morning matched her long, trailing scarf and was at least three sizes too big for her head.

"That you were in an accident and then disappeared for three days. And that some good samaritan found you and left you at the emergency room, but you can't remember what happened in between."

"Well," Lucy gave a thin smile, "that about sums it up." She waited for Dakota to grill her for more details, but the girl merely pointed at a series of large colorful posters hanging along the corridor.

"I don't suppose you'd be interested in being on my team?" Dakota asked.

Lucy drew a blank. "What team?"

"The Holiday Treasure Hunt. It's a scavenger hunt, really. The whole senior class divides into teams, and we all compete for prizes. Very big tradition here at Pine Ridge High."

"And is this tradition as important as the Fall Festival?"

"Well, it depends on what you're into, doesn't it?" Dakota proceeded to wrap her muffler numerous times around her neck as Lucy followed her into homeroom. The two took their desks near the window, and Lucy turned her attention to the snowy landscape outside.

It had taken herculean effort to shut off her mind, to not rehash again and again the disturbing events of last night. Luckily, Irene had gotten home within twenty minutes of Matt's departure, but Lucy still hadn't been able to sleep. She'd tossed and turned for hours, trapped in answerless questions and startled at every sound. When she'd finally gotten up and seen herself in the mirror—ghost-white skin and tired hollow eyes—she'd actually found herself wondering if she'd been in another wreck.

Dakota had been tactful enough not to even mention Lucy's haggard appearance. She'd merely stopped by Lucy's locker to ask if she felt better this morning, making casual small talk, putting Lucy at ease, smiling that Mona Lisa smile of hers. At least that's how Lucy had begun to think of it—that slight, mysterious curve to Dakota's lips that hinted of secrets known but never shared. Now, as Mr. Parkin took attendance, Lucy turned and shifted her attention to the desk behind her. Dakota was wearing knee-patched overalls again, fuzzy socks with beat-up sandals, and a leather bombadier's jacket. Between the layers of scarf and the droopy hat, Lucy couldn't even see the girl's eyes.

Like most of the class, Lucy drifted through the morning announcements. Despite her best intentions, she could feel paranoia creeping in again, as her eyes darted around the room, as she wondered how many of her classmates might have conspired against her to set up last night's charade. Was it just her imagination or was everyone trying not to look at her? Were kids smirking at each other, trying not to laugh? And had Dakota been telling the truth about what people really knew? The girl seemed to have a handle on things here at Pine Ridge High—if there were any other rumors going around, Lucy sensed that Dakota would be honest about them.

The bell rang again, signaling first period. As everyone spilled out into the hallway, Dakota tugged on Lucy's sleeve.

"See there?" she mumbled.

Lucy saw. Matt was standing just outside the administration office, jotting in a notebook, and talking earnestly with a small cluster of female students.

Dakota tugged her arm again. "There hasn't been this much sexual excitement around here since Mr. Enright took over the chemistry lab."

"Are you talking about Matt? I mean . . . *Father* Matt?" she quickly corrected herself.

Dakota's tone was solemn. "I have to admit— he's very hot."

"He's also a priest."

"That doesn't mean he's dead."

Lucy opted for another look. Matt was all business again today—properly religious from head to toe. Yet those faint streaks of sunlight still showed in his hair, and his grin was still easy and warm, and his eyelashes still lay long and thick against the fading tan of his cheeks.

For the first time Lucy really noticed the vast number of girls in the hall, moving at a snail's pace despite the sound of the bell. It was obvious from their faces that holy vows of any kind were not uppermost in their thoughts at the moment.

"So are you trying to tell me he's your type?" Lucy couldn't help teasing.

"No. I'm just trying to tell you that's he's too hot to be a priest."

"As hot as Mr. Enright?"

"Hotter. Mr. Enright's gay."

As the girls continued to watch him, Matt suddenly glanced up, recognized Lucy, and waved. Immediately heads began to swivel in her direction. Embarrassed, Lucy took Dakota's arm and moved her rapidly down the hall.

"He's nice, though," Dakota observed. "And he looked kind of worried about you."

"I . . . he's just trying to help me through some stuff. You know . . . like he's trying to help everyone else."

"Well, I'm glad he took you home yesterday. You shouldn't have tried to drive by yourself."

Lucy felt a tiny ripple of uneasiness. "How'd you know he took me home?"

They'd reached their classroom by now. Dakota paused outside the door and began unwinding her scarf.

"Come on, this school can't be *that* different from your old one. You know how information gets around. And besides"—she leaned forward with a conspiratorial whisper—"you can't expect to keep something a secret when Father Matt announces it to the whole office."

"It's not a secret," Lucy insisted. But it *did* help explain all the weird looks she'd been getting this morning. And maybe it explained something else, as well . . .

The whole office . . . the whole school. Which means anyone *could have found out I was alone yesterday. Anyone could have planned to scare me,* anyone *could have put that stuff in the car. Just a cruel joke. Just a mean trick, like Matt said.*

But what about the call from Angela? Could someone have managed to sneak into the house? Tamper with the fuse box? Rig the telephone somehow? Imitate Angela's voice?

Please let it be that. Please let it all be just a trick.

146

"Ladies, you're not going to learn anything lounging out here in the hall. Except, perhaps, bad posture."

As the teacher's voice broke into her thoughts, Lucy jerked back to the present. Dakota was already halfway through the door, and Mr. Timms was motioning Lucy to follow.

"Sorry," Lucy mumbled. She slid quickly into her seat, trying to figure out what the biology assignment had been for today. She couldn't even remember now if there'd been homework last night, much less if she'd done it.

She watched as Mr. Timms began listing various body parts on the board. At the next table over, Dakota was digging through her knapsack, the brim of her baggy hat practically obscuring her eyes.

Lucy took out her notebook. She hadn't even begun to catch up on all the schoolwork she'd missed so far; she didn't have the slightest idea how she was ever going to manage it. Not with so many tests looming on the horizon, and definitely not in her current state of mind. Sighing deeply, she clicked her pen, opened her notebook, and flipped to the next blank page.

And that's when her heart stopped.

For an endless moment her heart stopped beating, and the blood chilled solid in her veins.

She could see the words scrawled there, in large messy letters.

In strokes that had dried to a dark reddish brown.

Words meant for her . . .

And for her alone.

VERY SOON, LUCY

15

"Please—isn't there *any* way I can get in to see him?"

Lucy stood in the office, shifting anxiously from one foot to the other. She watched as the secretary consulted a schedule. Lucy clutched her notebook tight against her chest.

The woman looked up with a regretful smile. "I'm sorry, but—"

"It's very important. *Please*. *Very* important."

"What I'm trying to tell you is that Father Matt's left for the day. But the other grief counselers are still here. Perhaps you'd like to speak with Father Paul? Or Dr. Kauffman?"

"No. No . . . I . . ." Lucy stood for a moment, unsure what to do. Her mind felt blank. The notebook felt heavy in her arms. "Thanks anyway," she mumbled.

"I can schedule you for tomorrow," the secretary offered, but Lucy was already out in the hall.

Maybe this was a bad idea after all, showing this to Matt. Because what could Matt do about it anyway? Calm her down again? Try to convince her it was just another spiteful joke? And maybe it was, Lucy argued with herself. Maybe it *was* just another vicious prank. If she freaked out about it, then whoever had done this awful thing would win—again.

But what if it's not?

And what does it mean?

Had she been right about her unknown captor following her back to Pine Ridge? Knowing where she lived? Taunting her with those things in Angela's car? He could have found her notebook in the house last night and written his message then. And if she *was* right, who was going to help her? Who was going to protect her? If the police and the doctors hadn't believed her before, they *certainly* weren't going to believe her now.

How she longed for someone—*anyone*—to believe her.

Her resolve to keep silent had weakened with last night's incident. Her determination to handle things on her own had become shaky. Matt had listened to her, stayed with her, offered halfway sensible explanations—and though she'd been thoroughly frustrated at the time, it had felt so wonderful to have the burden lifted and shared, if even for just an hour or so.

She wasn't sure how much longer she could go on like this. Recalling the real-life nightmares. Struggling to stay sane. Feeling so terrified.

Being so alone.

But if she broke down and confided in Matt, would *he* die, too? Like Katherine? Like Byron? And what could she tell Matt, really? What could she expect from him if she didn't even know what she was dealing with?

Oh, Byron, I'd give anything to have you back again.

More depressed than ever, Lucy stopped at her locker. There wasn't anything she could do about the notebook now. She'd have to deal with it later—decide in the meantime whether or not to show it to Matt. She was late for class as it was. The bell for second period had already rung, and the corridor was deserted. She threw her notebook inside and was fumbling with the combination lock, when she heard laughter and running on the stairs.

The cheerleaders were late for practice, Lucy supposed. The whole uniformed group of them, with pom-poms in hand, making a beeline for the door at the end of the hall. Lucy drew back as they passed, and her eyes immediately landed on the girl with the short-cropped hair.

Wanda Carver.

She's going to die on Thursday.

Lucy's heart pounded. She felt herself step forward. Lift her arm to wave. Open her mouth to speak.

On Thursday.

She stood and watched the cheerleaders head off toward the gym. Her hands were shaky as she rechecked the door of her locker, tested the lock just one more time to make certain it was secure.

What am I thinking? I must be crazy.

Trying hard to compose herself, Lucy walked

slowly to class. She got a lecture for being tardy and flunked a test she'd completely forgotten to study for.

She didn't know if she could survive school until the weekend.

And it was only Tuesday.

16

I'm going to show Matt the notebook.

Lucy sat in the kitchen, both elbows on the table, chin propped in her hands.

No, I'm not.

Yes, I am.

She'd struggled with the decision all day. She hadn't been able to concentrate on anything else. And when school was finally over, she'd half expected the notebook to be missing from her locker, just like the jacket and blanket from Angela's car.

But it was still there, right where she'd left it. She'd shoved it down in her backpack, wedged it in tight, as though by trapping it there, she could end all the torture once and for all.

It was after six now. Irene hadn't come home yet, and as Lucy hunted for a memo pad, she kept glancing over at her backpack by the door. She didn't want to touch that notebook again, at least not till Matt had seen it. She didn't even want it in her room. As soon as Matt read the ominous message, she planned on throwing the notebook away. She could always copy Dakota's notes later.

In fact, that's where she was going tonight—to the bookstore to study with Dakota . . .

"I can't believe your aunt leaves you alone so much," Dakota had told her that afternoon. She'd insisted on giving Lucy a ride home, and they'd been on their way to the parking lot. "Don't you two ever do anything together?"

Lucy's laugh had been humorless. "She hardly even talks to me. And since Angela's been gone, she's been more distant than ever. She keeps Angela's room closed up. And all she does is work."

"Aren't you scared to be there by yourself?"

"Sometimes." But then, as Dakota's eyes had searched hers, Lucy had given in. "Actually . . . most of the time."

"I'm sorry."

Lucy had tried to smile. "The weird thing is, I was never afraid before. We lived in the city, in a walk-up apartment, and there were lots of times I stayed alone. My mom was a teacher. Sometimes she had school things to do at night, or meetings kept her late. It just never bothered me."

"There's my truck," Dakota had said.

It was big and old and clunky and even more beat-up than Dakota's knapsack. It had probably been cherry-red once, beneath all the dents and rust and scratches. And there was an odd assortment stowed in the back—a toolbox without a lid, two fishing poles, a laundry basket full of books, a gasoline can, and a small wicker rocking chair tied down with rope.

When Lucy tugged on the passenger door, Dakota had given it a hard shove from inside.

"Tragedies change us, don't they?" The girl's look had been intense as Lucy settled beside her. "We're never the same people we were before."

How true, Lucy thought now, climbing into Angela's car. She mentally reviewed the directions Dakota had given her and headed into town.

As her friend had predicted, the snow had all but disappeared, leaving streets and sidewalks a wet, muddy mess. Lucy drove slowly, watching for landmarks and street signs on the way. She'd never actually visited Pine Corners—the old section of Pine Ridge—and though a lot of places were open tonight, they didn't appear very busy. The four-block area allowed only foot traffic; there were parking lots at each end and curb parking in nearby neighborhoods. After several trips around the perimeter, Lucy finally found a spot on one of the adjacent streets, then set off briskly to find the bookstore.

Souvenir shops . . . art galleries and local crafts stores . . . cafés and coffee shops and an all-night diner—Lucy passed row after row of charmingly restored buildings, keeping a lookout for the alley she was supposed to take. There were a lot of alleyways, in fact, each of them quaintly named and squeezed inconspicuously between shops, where Lucy could glimpse tiny courtyards and miniature gardens beyond. After making a turn onto Candlewick Lane, she finally found the bookstore. It looked older than the other buildings—narrow, two stories high, and not nearly as well kept—but the door and windows and droopy awnings sparkled with strands of tiny white fairy lights, giving the place an almost magical quality. A curious assortment of lawn furniture and statues filled the small enclosure—stone elves and birdbaths, gargoyles and angels, all adorned with the same twinkling decor. And hanging from a clothesline were thirteen wind chimes, clanging out the most discordant harmony she'd ever heard.

Opening the door, Lucy went in. The first thing that struck her was the smell. A warm, musty smell of worn bindings and brittle pages, old leather and aged wood, damp wool coats and wet shoes, dust, a hint of mildew, and the strong rich smell of coffee.

The second thing she noticed were the books. Books everywhere. Shelves of books, tables of books, books stacked in corners, piled carelessly on the floor. Overstuffed chairs holding books instead of people. Books on the front counter and the rolltop desk behind it, and books on the staircase at the back of the room.

"Welcome to the eighth wonder of the world," said a familiar voice.

Turning, Lucy saw Dakota standing beside her, balancing a stack of books in her arms.

"I've never seen anything quite like it," Lucy agreed.

"Yes. We work very hard to maintain our reputation for clutter. Oh—Lucy, this is my dad."

Lucy instantly saw the resemblance. Though very tall and lanky, with wire-rimmed glasses and an absentminded smile, Mr. Montana had the same red hair and blue eyes as his daughter. He welcomed her to the store, encouraged her to get some coffee, and made her promise to come back again. Then, as a telephone rang, he obligingly transferred Dakota's books, excused himself, and hurried away.

Dakota raised an eyebrow at Lucy. "He'll tell you the exact same things next time you come, so don't be offended. He never remembers anybody."

"I like him. He seems really sweet."

"He is, but he makes me crazy. Come on—I'll give you the grand tour."

Dumping her coat and backpack behind the counter, Lucy followed Dakota through the rest of the shop. There were two more equally cramped rooms downstairs, and Dakota kept up a running dialogue as the two of them tried to maneuver their way around browsing customers and through tightly packed aisles.

"We try to categorize everything," Dakota explained, pointing things out as they went. "Keep all the genres together, make things easy for customers to find. But we just don't have enough space."

Lucy could see what she meant. Shelves bowed beneath their heavy loads, and baseboards were lined with boxes overflowing their contents.

"We're already double-shelving, so the rows are two books deep. And people hardly ever put stuff back where it belongs. So lots of titles end up in the wrong places."

"How do you keep track of everything?" Lucy asked in amazement.

"We don't. If we ever tried to clean behind those shelves, I bet we'd find books that have been missing for years."

The second-floor rooms, though every bit as crammed with books, were far less occupied with people. The light seemed dimmer up here; the rooms more stale and cold. There wasn't space enough for even one chair.

"What's that?" Lucy asked, pointing to a door with a KEEP OUT sign.

"Oh, that goes to the attic. We have a little office up there, but mostly it's just more books."

"Impossible."

"My mom keeps talking about moving to a bigger place. A newer store." Tilting her head, Dakota straightened the lopsided sign. "My dad keeps holding out for character and atmosphere."

"Do they both work here?"

"My dad, full-time. He's a writer, so this is perfect for him when business is slow. My mom's an artist. In fact you probably passed her gallery on your way. It's about five doors down."

Lucy was impressed. "It must be great to have such a creative family."

"Not if you're the only one who's not creative."

"Come on, I don't believe that."

"It's true. My sister's an awesome photographer; my brother's in a rock band and writes his own music. I'm the middle sibling who got *completely* passed over when it came to talent."

"There must be something you like. Something you're passionate about."

Dakota nodded. One corner of her mouth tugged down, and her pale eyes narrowed in thought.

"There is something," she admitted.

"Well, tell me. What is it?"

"You'll think I'm strange." Dakota hesitated, then sighed. "But then, of course, I *am* a bit strange, so you would be right."

Lucy couldn't help smiling. "Just tell me."

"In here."

Abruptly the girl turned and led Lucy into the last of the upstairs rooms. This room was easily the smallest of them all, with an odd configuration of shelving much like a maze, reaching from floor to ceiling and completely obscuring the windows, with unexpected turns and dead ends, and no rhyme or reason whatsoever.

"This is my favorite place," Dakota said quietly. "This is my passion."

She leaned against the door frame as Lucy took a cautious step into the room. For several long minutes Lucy was silent, her eyes sweeping back and forth over the hundreds of titles around her.

"Do all these deal with the supernatural?" Lucy finally asked. A tiny chill crept through her, raising goose bumps on her arms.

"Some people call it supernatural. Some call it real."

"What do *you* call it?"

Dakota moved slowly into the room. Her expression was thoughtful as she ran one hand along a row of old books.

"Lucy, there are just so many things out there that can't be explained or understood—not by our limited human perceptions, anyway. But those things still exist. They still happen. People are still affected by them . . . destinies are still controlled by them."

"Is that what you believe, then—that our destinies are predetermined?"

"I believe in everything." A thin smile flitted over Dakota's face. "But the question is . . . what do *you* believe in?"

"I . . . I guess I never thought about it."

"Witches? Zombies? Ghosts?"

Lucy pretended to be studying some titles. Adamantly she shook her head. "I really don't know much about any of that stuff."

"But you must have wondered about *something* in your life, right? Hasn't anything ever happened to you that was just too bizarre for this world?"

Lucy's eyes shot to the girl's face. "Why would you say that?"

"Vampires? Werewolves? Spells and curses? Just because you can't see what's in front of you doesn't mean it's not there."

The chill spread to Lucy's heart. She was wearing warm clothes, but she was beginning to shiver.

"No," she heard herself say. "No, I guess nothing like that's ever happened to me."

"Oh, well." Dakota seemed totally comfortable

with Lucy's reaction. "I warned you, you'd think I'm strange."

"I don't. I don't think that."

"This is the problem I face with my particular passion, you see. It doesn't involve any sort of creative talent, and I happen to be the only one who believes in it."

Still stunned by Dakota's revelations, Lucy watched her leave the room. *Tell her. Tell her the truth. Maybe she'll believe you. Maybe she'll have some insights . . . maybe she'll know how to help.* But Lucy couldn't say a word. Instead she could only stand there, trapped in a curious web of longing and denial.

"Lucy, are you coming?" Dakota was poised in the doorway, watching her. "I guess we've put off studying long enough."

The two went back downstairs. Dakota cleared off a lumpy, well-worn couch by the front window while Lucy poured each of them a cup of strong coffee from the pot on the counter. Then the girls settled themselves at opposite ends of the sofa, with their notes and textbooks spread out between them.

Somewhere between lists of required book

reports and unsolvable math problems, Lucy's attention began to wander. From time to time, she caught herself glancing over at Mr. Montana scribbling at his desk, or at the big round wall clock creeping interminably toward nine, or at Dakota's head bent low over yet another school project. The shop was practically empty now. Through the half-fogged window, she had a clear view of the courtyard beyond.

"You're drifting," Dakota mumbled, without looking up. "Only two more pages, I promise. Pay attention."

"Sorry."

"Don't be. It's incredibly boring."

Amused, Lucy tried her hardest to focus on the subject at hand. Dakota kept up a monotonous translation of French verbs. The bookstore was quiet now, and despite her megadose of caffeine, Lucy could feel herself getting drowsy. Her eyelids were heavy. With a halfhearted effort, she forced them open again and stared sleepily out the window.

Night lay deep within the courtyard walls. Like diminutive candle flames, the fairy lights glimmered softly through the shadows. The shadows where someone stood watching.

His face was near the glass.

Staring in at her.

And he looked just as she remembered, just as he had the last time she'd seen him, except for the bloodless pallor of his skin and his blank, hollow eyes.

"Oh God . . ."

She felt herself trying to stand. Trying to rise from the couch, trying to hold herself up and lean forward on shaky, unsteady legs . . .

"Lucy?" Dakota broke off in the middle of a sentence, looking up at her with a quizzical frown. "Lucy, what is it?"

And Lucy's voice trembled out, no more than a whisper.

"It's Byron."

17

"*What?*"

The book fell from Dakota's hands. As she jumped off the couch and reached out for Lucy, her eyes shot straight to the window.

"*What! Where?*"

But Lucy didn't hear. She was frozen helplessly in place, unaware of anything now but a misty pane of glass and shimmering pinpricks of light and a blanket of nighttime shadows in the courtyard just outside . . .

The deserted courtyard outside.

"I—" From some dreamlike place, she felt Dakota trying to pull her down again. "Didn't you see him?"

"Lucy, there's nobody out there."

"No, there *is*. *Was!* I *saw* him!"

"Lucy?" Dakota tugged at her again. "Come

on, sit down. Let me get you some fresh coffee."

But Lucy brushed her aside and ran for the door. Ignoring a startled glance from Mr. Montana, she hurried out to make a hasty search of the courtyard. A raw breeze swept down the alley, stinging through her clothes. It snaked through the wind chimes and played a macabre melody.

"Byron?" Lucy called.

You're losing your mind; you know Byron's dead.

Yet she'd seen someone there.

She'd seen *Byron* there.

Lucy rushed from the courtyard and back out through the alley. She looked frantically in every direction, but the shops were all closed, as still and deserted as the sidewalks.

And then she saw him.

He was at least fifty feet ahead of her, head bowed, walking rapidly toward the corner. She could see his dark hair blowing wild across his shoulders, and the long, easy stride of his legs . . .

"Byron!"

Before she even realized it, she was following

him, racing along the pavement, oblivious to the cold.

He was turning the corner now.

For one split second Lucy saw him hesitate, as though he might look back at her. He seemed to be listening to the pounding of her footsteps. Then he lowered his head again and disappeared.

"Byron!"

Lucy ran faster.

As she came around the corner, she could see that Byron was moving faster, as well. His shoulders were hunched against the wind, his collar turned high around his neck. He cut across a parking lot, then headed for a gap between two buildings. It was all Lucy could do to keep up.

Her breathing was ragged; her chest burned from the cold. As she entered the narrow opening, she caught a shadowy glimpse of Byron at the other end of the alley. Once more he paused, but just for an instant, before stepping out into the dim light of a streetlamp beyond.

"Byron! Wait!"

Lucy burst from the passageway, her heart ready to explode.

And then she stood there, staring in disbelief. The figure had vanished.

From end to end, as far as she could see, the area was completely deserted.

"No . . . no . . . it's impossible . . ."

She seemed to be in some sort of delivery zone. To her left stood a row of identical buildings, small loading docks, and Dumpsters, obviously back entrances to shops and restaurants. To her right was a fenced-in wooded area, which she guessed to be a park. The high spiked gates were chained with a padlock; there were benches and overgrown pathways inside.

Maybe he climbed the fence. Maybe he left through the park. Yet Lucy doubted he'd had enough time to cover that much distance before she'd come out of the alley.

My God, just listen to yourself.

She was talking about Byron as if he'd deliberately led her here. As if he'd deliberately eluded her.

She was talking about Byron as if he were still alive.

But I saw him. I saw him!

Lucy strained her ears through the darkness. The wind had gone still. It was so unnervingly quiet, she could hear the echo of her own heartbeat.

So quiet . . .

Too quiet.

Suddenly she wanted to get away from here. For the first time it dawned on her just how foolish she'd been to follow some shadowy figure into an isolated part of town. He wasn't Byron—of *course* he wasn't Byron! And now he could be anywhere—*close* to her—*watching* her. The one in the cave . . . the one in her nightmares . . . the one nobody ever believed existed . . .

Lucy turned and ran back.

Back through the alley, back to the sidewalk, where she saw Dakota standing on the corner and looking frantic, trying to figure out where Lucy had gone.

"Lucy! Thank God!"

There was relief in Dakota's voice. Relief and fear mixed together, as the girl ran up to her and caught her in a hug. "Are you okay?"

"I saw him, Dakota. I'm not crazy."

"No, but you're frozen. Come back inside."

"It was Byron."

"We'll talk about it."

Reluctantly, Lucy allowed Dakota to lead her to the bookshop, where Mr. Montana was waiting for them at the door. He handed each of the girls a refill of hot coffee, then tactfully retreated to his desk.

"Sit down." Dakota steered her firmly to the couch. "Drink this. And don't try to tell me anything till you stop shaking."

But Lucy was too upset to follow orders. "I'm sorry," she blurted out. "I . . . I know it sounds impossible—"

"No. It doesn't."

"I know it sounds *insane*, but I really think it was him."

"It doesn't sound insane."

"Well, of *course*, it sounds insane, Dakota. *Byron's dead!*"

Dakota sat beside her. She propped her elbows on her knees and wrapped both hands around her cup. She blew gently on her coffee. She stared thoughtfully at the floor. "If you believe it's real," she said at last, "then it's real."

Lucy's tone was bitter. "But haven't you heard? I hit my head in the accident. I have flashbacks and I forget things. I'm prone to delusions, and I make things up. Most of the time, I don't even know what I'm talking about."

"That's crap."

Surprised, Lucy watched as Dakota looked up, took a cautious sip of coffee, then turned to face her.

"You are not delusional," Dakota said calmly. "You are brave. And you are gifted. And I am certainly not the person who's going to think you're imagining things."

Lucy hadn't expected this. It was such a shock and such a relief that quick tears sprang to her eyes. For a long moment, she couldn't even speak.

"Weren't you listening to a single thing I said upstairs?" Dakota went on. "I told you, I believe in everything."

"But you told me you didn't see anyone out in the courtyard."

"I didn't. But that doesn't mean *you* didn't." Dakota blew on her coffee again. "Reality's in the eye of the beholder."

"But what if you don't *know* what's real any-more?"

Dakota's gaze was steady and serene. "*You know*, Lucy. You have an aura about you . . . a special kind of energy I've never felt before. Except from one other person."

Mystified, Lucy stared at her. Dakota reached out and squeezed Lucy's hand.

"Byron," Dakota said softly. "I felt it with Byron. He had a gift, and so do you. Only yours is much, much stronger. Maybe even stronger than you realize."

18

"Dakota . . . what are you saying?"

A hint of a smile crossed Dakota's face. She tucked her legs beneath her and settled back against the cushions.

"I remember the first time I saw Byron," Dakota explained. "He came into the bookstore, and the whole atmosphere changed."

"I don't understand."

"I told you . . . it's like this individual energy that every person gives off. I didn't know Byron then, but when he walked through that door, it was like a physical shift in the air. I knew there was something very different . . . very special . . . about him. But I never knew what."

Lucy gave a curt nod. She was fascinated by Dakota's observations and wanted to hear more.

"I'd heard stories about his sister, of course—being psychic, being a witch, being a fortune-teller. But people turn cruel when they don't understand someone. And Byron was really protective of her. So I didn't pay much attention to all the rumors."

Lucy felt tension building inside her. The temptation to blurt everything out, to reveal everything to Dakota was suddenly unbearable. Through sheer willpower, she forced her emotions down again, kept her face impassive, focused on Dakota's narrative.

"But with Byron," Dakota continued, "something was definitely there."

"But . . . you don't know what it was."

"No." Dakota took a sip of coffee. "But I think *you* do."

Lucy looked out the window. She could hear the scrape of Mr. Montana's chair, could hear him going through the shop turning off lights. She felt Dakota lean forward again on the couch.

"Lucy, trust your instincts," Dakota said urgently. "Don't let anyone tell you they're not true."

Without waiting for a reply, Dakota began gathering up their books and papers. It was almost as if nothing out of the ordinary had happened tonight, and Lucy sat for a few minutes longer, letting it all sink in.

"Dad and I are stopping for something to eat," Dakota finally said. "Why don't you come with us?"

"No, I really can't. But thanks."

"Are you going to be okay?"

Still avoiding eye contact, Lucy nodded. "I'm okay."

"Then we'll at least give you a ride to your car."

Lucy was glad for the escort. This old section of Pine Ridge reminded her of a ghost town now, and her car was the only one in the lot.

"Be careful going home," Dakota warned her. "There's a bunch of one-way streets around here, and it's easy to get turned around."

Lucy watched the Montanas drive off. She let the motor idle and waited for the heater to warm up. Her thoughts were clamoring for attention, but she couldn't sort them out. All she could concentrate on was the fact that

Dakota hadn't asked for any explanations, hadn't expected any confidences, hadn't questioned her sanity.

Dakota had believed her.

Hadn't she?

Lucy rested her cheek on the steering wheel. It had been so long since she'd felt validated by anyone that suspicions began creeping in. Maybe Dakota was just pretending. Maybe she was just some weirdo who enjoyed acting out supernatural fantasies. Maybe she was just trying to get close to Lucy so she could play another cruel trick on her.

Yet Lucy didn't think so.

"Trust your instincts . . . don't let anyone tell you they're not true."

And Lucy's instincts were telling her now that Dakota believed her. That Dakota was a friend.

Sitting up straight, Lucy adjusted the heater and switched on her headlights. Then she pulled onto the street and started for home.

It didn't take her long to realize she was lost.

Landmarks started looking way too familiar, and after an endless series of frustrating turns, Lucy saw that she'd been going in a complete circle. *Come on, don't panic—after all, this is a small town . . .*

She tried to recall the exact sequence of street names Dakota had given her. But despite her best efforts, Lucy eventually found herself in a neighborhood of run-down houses and broken streetlights, with no clue as to how she'd gotten there.

Damn! Swearing under her breath, she looked for a place to turn around. The houses were spaced wide apart, the yards neglected and overgrown, with wide patches of shadows in between. As she started into a driveway, a dog suddenly lunged toward the car, barking furiously. Lucy jerked the wheel hard to the left. She felt the car swerve, then bump noisily over something piled along the curb. To her relief, she spotted a cul-de-sac at the end of the street and immediately stepped on the gas.

One house stood alone in the cul-de-sac. An old Victorian surrounded by tall trees and clipped hedges and a picket fence without a gate. Though it had definitely seen better days, it looked more well kept than the other houses on the block, and a porch light cast a welcoming glow over the leaded glass in the front door.

Lucy couldn't help staring at it as she drove into the circle. She was still staring at it, in fact, when she suddenly became aware of the car leaning to one side and the slapping sound coming from underneath the front end.

Oh, no . . . don't tell me . . .

Shifting into park, Lucy jumped out and gazed in dismay at the flat tire.

Great. Now what am I supposed to do?

She didn't know how to change a tire. She didn't have a clue where any gas stations were, or if any were even open at this hour. And a flat tire hardly qualified as a 911 emergency. Grabbing her cell phone, she dialed Irene's number and let it ring. And ring. And ring. When the answering machine finally came on, Lucy left a message. Then she clicked off in disgust.

She couldn't just wait here all night—God only knew when her aunt would get home. She'd left Matt's phone number on her dresser, so that was useless; she'd left the business card Dakota had given her, too. And even if she called Information for the Montanas' home number, Dakota and her dad wouldn't be back yet anyway.

Totally frustrated, Lucy looked over at the isolated house. She didn't have a choice, really—there was only one thing to do.

Shutting off the car, she slammed the door and locked it.

Then she took a deep breath, squared her shoulders, and marched determinedly up the steps to the front porch.

19

There was a black wreath on the door.

Lucy hadn't noticed it from the street, because it was hidden in shadows. But now she could see the black crepe and black ribbons, the dried black flowers and tiny black jewels, all woven together in an intricate, antique design.

She'd seen something like this once before. But it had been a picture in a book—a black wreath hung upon a door, an old-fashioned custom to show that someone in the house had died.

Lucy hesitated. The last thing she wanted to do was intrude on a family's grief. If someone in this house had indeed died recently, maybe she should go somewhere else.

She was still trying to make up her mind when the door swung open.

Startled, Lucy found herself confronted by a tall, bony woman with a sour face, pointed chin, and frizzy gray hair. A starched apron was tied over her shapeless brown dress, and she was drying her hands on a dish towel.

"What is it?" the woman snapped.

Lucy quickly recovered herself. "I'm sorry to bother you, but—"

"I saw you lurking out here—don't you know what time it is? Well, whatever it is you're selling, I don't want it."

"I'm not selling anything. I'm just having car trouble."

The woman eyed her suspiciously. "Look at you. You been in some kind of wreck?"

"I . . ." Lucy's hand went self-consciously to the bruises on her face. "I . . . tripped on the stairs."

The woman considered this. Then she craned her neck and squinted toward the street. "Is that your car?"

"I've got a flat tire—I was wondering if I could use your phone book."

"A flat tire, you say? I don't see any flat tire."

"Yes, it's right there on the passenger side.

There in front." Lucy felt the woman's sharp gaze rake over her, head to foot. "Please. I just need someone to change it."

"Well, *I* can't change it. There's nobody here who can change it."

"I meant, I need to call someone."

"Why don't you call your parents?"

"I tried, but nobody's home."

"That's the trouble with kids these days. Parents never around when they should be."

Keeping respectfully silent, Lucy endured several more minutes of scrutiny. Then, apparently satisfied she wasn't going to be mugged by a desperate teenage girl, the woman motioned Lucy inside.

Despite the well-worn exterior of the house, the hall was clean and shiny. Lucy could smell floor wax and lemon polish and the faint scent of lavender as she was ushered into a small, snug living room. And though the furniture looked antiquated, there wasn't a speck of dust anywhere.

It didn't seem like a house where someone had died, Lucy thought. No flower arrangements, no stacks of sympathy cards, no all-pervasive feelings of sorrow and emptiness and despair. Maybe the people who lived here just liked black wreaths.

"Phone book's over there." The woman jerked her chin toward the far wall. "Phone, too. And don't be leaving any smudges on that desk."

"I won't. Thank you."

"What are you doing out this late anyway? Can't be anything good, young person out this late."

"I was on my way home and got lost. I was just trying to find somewhere to turn around."

"Hmmm. Turn around or scope out the neighborhood?"

Lucy ignored the accusation. "I haven't lived here very long. And I'm really bad with directions."

She walked over and picked up the phone book. The woman stood in the doorway and watched.

"Do you know who I could call?" Lucy asked politely. "A gas station? A garage?"

"What do you think this is, New York City? You're not going to find anyone this time of night. Everything's closed."

Lucy's heart sank. She laid the telephone book on the desk.

"Oh. Well . . . thanks anyway."

"Thanks for what? You didn't call anybody. And your tire's not fixed."

Lucy sighed. "Thanks for . . . letting me in."

But as she reached the front door, the woman stopped her. "Where do you think you're going?"

"My cell phone's in the car. I left a message on my aunt's machine—she might be trying to reach me."

"People talk too loud on those cell phones, act like they're the only ones in the world who have something to say. Well, let me tell you . . . nobody cares about hearing their business."

I should introduce you to Mr. Montana, Lucy thought, but aloud she said, "Well . . . I only use it for emergencies."

"So in the meantime you're just going to sit out there in the cold? Catch pneumonia? Get your purse snatched? Or worse?"

Lucy was getting irritated. It had been a long day, an emotional night, and she wasn't in the mood for any more upsets.

"It's not like I have many options," she replied, more sarcastically than she'd meant to.

The woman's lips pinched tight. "Come into the kitchen. Take off your coat, and put it in that closet. And for heaven's sake, hang it up neat."

Surprised, Lucy did as she was told. When she entered the kitchen, she saw gleaming countertops, a well-scrubbed, though outdated, stove, and a table with a blue flowered cloth. Pots of ivy lined the windowsill over the sink, and a large gray cat peered at her from beneath one of the straight-backed chairs.

"You like pie?" The woman's back was turned away from Lucy, bent inside a pantry, taking out dishes.

"I love pie."

"Then sit down. You don't eat pie very often, I can tell. Home cooking either. You're puny."

Lucy sat. She could feel the cat rubbing against her legs, could hear its loud purr of contentment.

"One more thing wrong with kids today," the woman went on. "Never have a decent meal. Never sit down as a family. Too many divorces."

Since she didn't get the feeling that she was expected to answer, Lucy kept quiet. She leaned down and scratched the cat behind its ears.

"There were ten of us when I was growing up. Dinnertime was nonnegotiable. We all had chores to do. Made us learn responsibility. Made us appreciate what we had."

Lucy watched as a pie was sliced, transferred to a plate, and shoved into the microwave. Within seconds, the warm fragrance of apples and cinnamon and buttery crust filled the room. She heard her stomach rumble. She'd forgotten just how hungry she was.

"Kids today expect handouts. Something for nothing, and right when they want it." Indignantly, the woman set a plate and fork down in front of Lucy. "Use that napkin there. And don't make crumbs all over the table."

It was the best pie Lucy had ever tasted. Flaky and sweet, it melted in her mouth and warmed her all the way down.

"This is wonderful," Lucy sighed, feeling almost as contented as the cat. "Really, this was just so nice of you. I didn't want you to go to any trouble."

"If it was trouble, I wouldn't have done it."

The woman pulled out a chair. She sat down across the table, took a tissue from her apron pocket, and dabbed it over her brow. Lucy swallowed another bite of pie.

"So you haven't lived here very long." The woman had obviously been thinking about this. "*How* long?"

"Just a few weeks."

"You go to church?"

"I . . . really haven't decided on a particular church yet."

"You should go to church. Young people today—no morals. No values. That's what happens when you don't go to church." She leaned toward Lucy with a frown. "There's a new priest at All Souls. He's too young to be a *good* priest, but with Father Paul having problems, we're stuck with him."

Lucy stared at her. "You mean Father Matt?"

"And how can I call him Father? It's like calling my grandson Father."

"I've met Father Matt," Lucy told her. "He's one of the grief counselors at my school."

"And what would he know about counseling

people? He hasn't lived long enough to counsel anybody."

Giving a noncommittal shrug, Lucy casually checked her watch. Where *was* Irene, anyway? What if she'd been home for hours and just hadn't checked her answering machine? *How long will it take her to realize I'm gone? How long will it take her to notice the time and—*

"So you didn't have time to know Byron, I guess."

Lucy's head came up. The woman's eyes were narrowed on her like lasers. The last bite of pie stuck in her throat, and she struggled to choke it down.

"As if his grandmother hasn't been through enough already," the woman added, not giving Lucy a chance to reply. "Well, it's not my place to say anything, is it? I'm just helping out. You've heard what you've heard at school already, so you know how he died in that wreck. But he was a good kid, not like most. Took care of his grandmother, just the two of them. Oh, there was an older girl once—mad as a March hare. But she took off, and no one's heard from her since."

A strange feeling of dread began to creep over Lucy. A feeling of secrets and doom, of being in the wrong place at the worst possible time.

"That's him there," the woman said, pointing. As Lucy's eyes moved to the refrigerator, she noticed for the first time a small photograph stuck to the door with a magnet. "That's Byron. Sad. He was such a good-looking boy."

Oh my God . . .

Lucy's throat was closing. Closing up around that wedged bit of food, so that she couldn't swallow, couldn't breathe. Her chest was squeezing. Her hands were frozen on the tabletop.

"This . . ." She could barely get the words out. "This . . . is his house?"

"Didn't you know?"

The woman got up and walked to the refrigerator. Lucy couldn't move, not even when the photograph was thrust in front of her.

"Well, I guess you *wouldn't* know," the woman concluded, "since you haven't lived here that long."

"You're Mrs. Dempsey," Lucy mumbled, and those flinty eyes bored into her once again.

"Have we met?"

"No. Father Matt told me you were staying with Byron's grandmother."

"She's bedridden. Stroke. Been that way for a long time. Oh, the nurse comes, but Mrs. Wetherly appreciates *little* things the nurse can't make time for. Fresh flowers every so often. Nice music. Being read to. Company when she's not too tired."

Mrs. Dempsey returned the photo to its rightful place. Then she studied Lucy with a pensive frown.

"In fact, maybe you should go back and see her. Since you're from Byron's school. Just to say hello."

The kitchen walls gave a crazy lurch, rocking the chair with them. Lucy held on tighter to the edge of the table.

"I don't want to bother her," she whispered.

"You won't. Come with me."

There was no getting out of it. As Lucy took the long walk down the hall, she felt like a prisoner bound for the execution chamber. She could see an open door at the end of the corridor. A glow of light spilling over the threshold, slanting across throw rugs on the floor.

Please, please, let her be asleep . . . please just let me slip out again without her ever knowing . . .

Lucy wanted to turn, to run—but she had images of Mrs. Dempsey grabbing her by the neck and throttling her into submission.

"In here," Mrs. Dempsey said. She stopped just inside the doorway, and Lucy could see the old-fashioned bed, and the mounds of fluffy white covers, and the soft, stacked pillows trimmed in lace.

"Odelia," Mrs. Dempsey announced, "here's one of Byron's friends to say hello."

The frail figure lying there seemed pitifully lost among the bed linens. As Lucy gripped the edge of the footboard, she could see how small Byron's grandmother was, how pale and still, her face a mass of wrinkles, her long braid of silver hair draped across one shoulder of her cream-colored nightgown.

But to Lucy's distress, Mrs. Wetherly wasn't asleep. In fact, her huge dark eyes, every bit as dark as Byron's had been, were directed toward the end of the bed, resting calmly on Lucy's face.

"She can hear you," Mrs. Dempsey advised Lucy in an undertone. "She can understand you, and she can move her left arm a little. But she can't talk. So she uses those things there."

She indicated a small slate and piece of chalk on the nightstand. Lucy managed a stiff nod.

"Well, go on," Mrs. Dempsey insisted, nudging her. "You can't visit clear across the room. Tell her your name."

But Lucy's feet were rooted to the floor. She tried to open her mouth. Her tongue was like cotton; her lips wouldn't move.

"Well, tell her your name, for heaven's sake. You expect her to read your mind?" As Byron's grandmother made a weak gesture, Mrs. Dempsey pushed Lucy forward. "Give her the chalk, and hold the slate so she can reach it."

Lucy felt sick. She crossed the short distance to the bed, wondering desperately what to do. She couldn't tell the truth—she just couldn't. That Byron had died was devastating enough. But that *she* was still alive, standing here in his grandmother's bedroom—that was just too horrible for anyone to bear.

The old woman's eyes had never left her. Even as Lucy picked up the stub of chalk and placed it in the blue-veined hand, those faded eyes continued to watch her, showing no hint of emotion. She heard the doorbell ring and fought a moment of panic as Mrs. Dempsey marched from the room.

But still the words refused to come. Words of comfort, words of remorse—though they tore at Lucy's heart and welled up into tears, she just couldn't bring herself to speak them aloud.

And then, to her amazement, Mrs. Wetherly's hand began to move.

Slowly . . . painstakingly . . . the old woman's fingers clawed around the chalk . . . motioned at the slate. Lucy lowered it in front of her. Held it tightly as the gnarled hand began to write.

The letters were like a child's letters. Crooked and crude, but clearly readable as they printed across the blank surface of the slate.

Lucy stared at them in silence. Four clumsy letters that she recognized at once.

L U C Y.

20

"Oh God," Lucy whispered. "Oh God . . . how did you know?"

The old woman's eyes looked deep into hers. In the dark fixed stare Lucy saw a sorrow that was endless . . . and a compassion that was immeasurable.

The sheer power of it left her breathless.

Unconsciously she took a step back, but before she could look away, Lucy saw something else.

Something forming in the depths of Mrs. Wetherly's eyes . . . something gazing back at her . . . haunting and achingly familiar . . .

Byron's face.

Byron's face trapped there in the dark . . .

"No," Lucy mumbled, "no, it's not possible . . ."

Somehow she made it out of the room and

down the hall. She snatched her coat from the closet, not even bothering to put it on. Fumbling with the lock on the front door, she didn't hear Mrs. Dempsey calling from the kitchen, wasn't aware of the footsteps approaching, until hands suddenly grabbed her shoulders and turned her around.

"Lucy!" Matt exclaimed. "What are you doing here?"

Lucy's head was throbbing, her eyes blurry with unshed tears. She jerked away from Matt and resumed her struggle with the door.

"Mrs. Dempsey told me someone had a flat tire, but I didn't know it was you." Reaching out, Matt pried her hands from the doorknob and took them in his own. "Lucy, it's not a problem. I'll be glad to give you another ride home."

"I don't want a ride home!" Lucy's thoughts were spinning—she couldn't get the image of Byron's face out of her mind. *It wasn't real—I just thought it was. Their eyes are the same, that's all. Just the eyes are the same, just the eyes, that's all it was, the rest of it was just in my mind.* "I'm sure Irene's called by now. I just need my phone. I need to get my phone from the car."

"I'll get your phone—you stay in here where it's warm. What a coincidence I happened to stop by at the same time you did."

"I didn't stop by. I didn't even *plan* to stop by. I never should have come inside, I never should have stayed. I want to go. I need to go!"

"You mean . . ."

Matt finally seemed to be comprehending the situation. For an instant he looked disconcerted.

"You didn't even know whose house this was, did you?" he asked her at last. "You didn't have a clue it was Byron's grandmother."

Lucy turned back to the door. *She knew me—how could she possibly have known me?* Shaking her head, Lucy kept silent. She heard Matt sigh deeply behind her.

"Right," Matt mumbled under his breath. "What are the odds?"

And I saw Byron . . . Byron in her eyes . . .

"Save that tea for me, will you Mrs. Dempsey?" Matt shrugged into his jacket and ushered Lucy out the front door, leaving the woman to stare after them in bewilderment.

"Lucy, I can't imagine what a shock that must

199

have been for you. How'd you end up here anyway?"

"I don't know," she answered miserably. "I kept taking wrong turns and hitting dead ends. And then I was on this street, and I saw the porch light."

"Let me take a look at that tire."

Lucy watched impatiently as Matt knelt down by the Corvette. But after a thorough inspection, he shook his head

"It's split wide open; you'll have to get a new one." He stood and brushed off the knees of his jeans. "Okay, two options. I can put your spare on right now, or I can take you home."

"Please. I just want to go."

"Then I'll call a tow truck for you in the morning, and you can pick it up sometime tomorrow. Glen's Repair over on Hawthorne Street. It's the one Father Paul uses, and that antique car of his still runs like a dream. So I figure this Glen guy must be some kind of miracle worker."

Lucy took her backpack from the car and locked the doors. Then she followed Matt to his Jeep and got in.

"How come you're out this late?" Matt asked curiously as they wound their way out of the neighborhood. "Not that this is *late*, of course— but late for Pine Ridge."

Lucy stared at the dashboard. The heater was on, but hadn't had a chance to warm up. Unconsciously, she held her hands out toward the vents.

"I was studying with a friend. Her family has this old bookstore in Pine Corners."

"Dakota Montana, right? Yeah, I've been to that bookstore—it's pretty amazing. You could spend hours poking around and still not see everything."

"I saw Byron," Lucy said.

Her eyes widened slowly as she realized what she'd said. *Oh God . . . why did I do that?*

From the corner of her eye, she caught Matt's quick glance. "You . . . what?"

Should she pursue it? Go into detail? Hadn't she acted crazy enough around Matt for one night?

"I was looking out the window. And I thought I saw Byron," she mumbled at last.

"Oh. You *thought* you saw him."

Lucy shut her eyes. "I *did* see him."

An uncomfortable silence settled between them. Lucy opened her eyes again, and focused on her outstretched hands. When Matt finally spoke, his voice was gentle.

"Where? Where'd you see him?"

"Don't talk to me like that."

Matt was surprised. "Like what?"

"Like you'd talk to some three-year-old with imaginary friends. I'm not making it up. And I'm not crazy."

"Lucy—"

"No. I'm tired of people not believing me. I'm tired of people treating me like I belong in a mental institution. And you know, it's all such bullshit. Everybody says *talk* about it—get it *out* so you can move on with your life. But when I *do* talk about it, everyone says oh dear, she's *hallucinating*. It's the *head* injury, it's the *pain* medication."

"Lucy—"

"Out of all the houses I could have picked to ask for help tonight, why was it *that* house? And do you know what happened when Mrs. Dempsey made me go into that bedroom?

Byron's grandmother *knew* me! She wrote my name on her slate! How could she know me, she's never even seen me before!"

"Well, maybe—"

"No. Just listen to me. If you don't believe when I *tell* you things, then maybe you'll believe something you can *see*. Maybe you'll believe *this*."

Furiously, Lucy dug into her backpack. She found the notebook she'd wedged in there earlier, and yanked it out, spilling papers all over the front seat. As Matt kept one eye on her and the other on the street, she started flipping through the pages.

"So you think it's all just in my mind? Then what do you think about solid proof? What do you think about messages written in blood?"

Matt pulled over to the curb. He put the Jeep in park and gave Lucy his full and silent attention. As Lucy kept turning the pages of the notebook, her movements grew more frantic. She got to the end, and a look of confusion struck her face. Immediately she began flipping backward, then forward again, then back. Jerking up the notebook, she turned it sideways and shook it violently, trying to dislodge any loose papers that might be stuck inside. Confusion turned to disbelief. Disbelief turned to desperation.

"Lucy," Matt said quietly.

"No! It was *here*! Someone put it in my notebook, and it was *here*! I *saw* it! It can't be gone—there's no *way* it could be gone! I had it with me every minute, and then I locked the car!"

But then she remembered.

She remembered placing her backpack behind the counter at the bookstore. Going off with Dakota for a tour. Not checking the backpack again when they'd sat down to study. Not checking again after she'd gone to search for Byron and Dakota had gone in search of her. Just assuming the notebook was still there, exactly where she'd left it.

"Someone must have taken it," she murmured now. "Someone must have taken it at the bookstore. That's the only place it could have happened."

But maybe it had happened while she was inside the Wetherly house. Maybe someone had broken into the car, then locked it up again. Anyone could do that . . . an expert could do that. Someone who enjoyed playing mean, cruel tricks could do that or . . .

Someone who follows me. Someone who watches. Someone who hides in the shadows of a cave . . .

She looked beseechingly at Matt. "It said, 'very soon.'"

And she suddenly realized that Matt had ahold of her hands and was leaning toward her, his brow creased with worry, his eyes full of sadness and sympathy.

"What did, Lucy?" he asked her.

"The message. The warning. It was in my notebook when I opened it this morning. It said, 'Very soon, Lucy.' And it was the color of dried blood. In fact, I'm *sure* it was dried blood—it *looked* like dried blood . . ."

Her voice trailed away. She felt Matt draw her closer, and as all the strength drained out of her, Lucy pressed her head against his chest.

"I don't know how it got there, Matt," she whispered. "And I don't know how it disappeared."

She closed her eyes and kept very still. She

could feel the warmth of his jacket and the strong beat of his heart. She could feel the steady vibration of the car, and the rush of heat from the vents.

She could feel Matt smoothing back her hair.

She could feel his arms starting around her, and his sudden hesitation, and the way he shifted away from her then, ever so slightly.

"Lucy." His voice was low. "I want you to have this."

Lucy drew back. She watched Matt reach up and remove a chain from around his neck. He stared at it for a moment, then eased it carefully over her head.

"What are you doing?" she asked, surprised.

The chain was thin, but sturdy. It slid into place, its small, round medallion resting lightly upon the front of her coat.

"Someone gave me this a long time ago." Matt smiled faintly, as though remembering. "It's helped me through some pretty rough times. Maybe you could give it a try."

"Oh, Matt . . ."

Lucy didn't know what to say. Lifting the medallion, she held it up close, trying to see the design. In the dim interior of the Jeep, it appeared to be carved with some sort of pattern, but one that Lucy didn't recognize.

"It's an ancient holy symbol," Matt explained.

"It's beautiful. But, Matt, I can't keep it."

"Why not?"

"Because it's special to you. You can't just give it to me like this."

"But I just did. And now I hope it'll be special to *you*."

Then, before Lucy could protest, he switched his attention to the steering wheel.

"Better get you home," he said quickly.

And it wasn't till much later, when Lucy was lying awake in bed, that she realized she'd never even asked him what the symbol meant.

21

She dreamed she was back at the tomb.

Back in the old cemetery, standing outside the Wetherly mausoleum.

She was alone.

And someone was following her.

In the nightmare, Lucy looked back over her shoulder, into the pitch-black night, through the wind-lashed trees, beyond the pounding rain. Thunder shook the ground beneath her feet. Thunder loud enough to wake the dead.

She pressed her face against the wrought-iron gates of the family crypt. The gates were locked, but she wrapped her hands tightly around the tall spikes and began to pull. Lightning flashed overhead, throwing the graveyard in and out of shadow. And with every stab of lightning, she caught just a glimpse of the tomb's cold interior, the leaf-littered floor, and the catacombed walls.

Terror rose inside her. The terror of being stalked, the terror of imminent danger.

The rain fell harder.

The air reeked of death.

Without any warning, the gates swung open. Yet Lucy remained on the crumbling steps, powerless to move.

"Byron," she called, "Byron, please help me!"

And then a voice—*his* voice—faint and sad and empty, from somewhere she couldn't see . . .

"Keep away," he warned her. "There's no one in this place."

Lucy shot up in bed.

Her heart was racing, and her nightgown was damp with sweat.

As she tossed back her covers, the last bits and pieces of dreaming clutched at her mind before fading and vanishing altogether.

She was out of breath. She swung her feet to the floor and padded barefoot to the sliding glass doors, parting the curtains and gazing out at the darkness.

Snow flittered against a velvet backdrop of night.

The pane felt icy to her touch, yet her body pulsed with heat.

That ache again.

That deep, insistent ache that made her want to moan, that ache that couldn't be filled.

Slowly she drew her nightgown off over her head.

She pressed her naked body to the glass, savoring the smooth, shocking cold against her skin.

How she longed to be out in that darkness.

Out beyond the backyard wall . . . out beyond those trees shining silver beneath the moon . . .

For some weird, unknown reason, the longing to be outside was suddenly—almost painfully—overwhelming.

Lucy started to unlock the doors, then remembered the security system was on. If only she could step out to the balcony, feel the snowflakes on her cheeks, the wind through her hair. The room was getting warmer; the walls were closing in. She couldn't stand being here one more second. Grabbing her robe from the foot of the bed, she slipped it on and tiptoed through the silence of the house.

She paused to disarm the security system. Her breath was coming faster now, her heart fluttering in anticipation. As though she were bound for some forbidden rendezvous. As though the night were her secret lover.

Without a sound, Lucy crept out the back door.

The wind loosened the sash at her waist, blowing her robe open and easing it down off her shoulders. It whipped around her as she spread her arms wide and embraced the cold.

Stimulating . . . invigorating . . . it made her feel strangely alive.

As though sorrow had never touched her . . .

As though she *belonged* somewhere . . .

"Lucy? What in heaven's name are you doing?"

The voice came from behind her. Startled, Lucy hastily tied her robe together and turned to see Irene hovering in the kitchen doorway.

"Lucy," her aunt asked again, but more puzzled than angry, "*what* are you doing out here?"

"I . . ."

Lucy stared back in confused silence. Irene obviously expected some sort of answer from her, but the longer Lucy stared, the more she began to realize that she didn't actually *know* what she was doing out here. Out here in the cold and the snow, in the middle of the night.

"I . . . needed some air."

It was the only thing her brain could come up with on such short notice. She shivered violently and realized she had nothing on her feet.

"Come back inside." Irene's frown was colder than the temperature. "Honestly, Lucy, this makes me wonder if Dr. Fielding should increase your medication. Instead of acting so foolishly, why didn't you just adjust the thermostat?"

Lucy took the scolding in her stride.

She went back to her room, donned a pair of flannel pajamas, and piled more blankets on the bed.

And then she stood there in the darkness,

peering out through the sliding glass doors, hugging herself against the chill that lingered in her veins.

She stared off across the lawn and past the low stone wall, and she realized that something had changed.

Something about the night.

Something that made it different now . . . different in a way she couldn't quite understand.

Almost as though it had been alive before . . .

But now, it was only a dream.

22

"You haven't said three words since we sat down," Dakota chided gently. "And you haven't touched your lunch."

Startled from her reverie, Lucy gave her friend a guilty look. "Sorry. I just don't have much of an appetite, I guess."

"I guess, too," Dakota echoed. "Lucy, you have to start eating better—you need to keep up your strength." Then, when Lucy didn't respond, she added, "Are you still worried about your notebook? I'll ask my dad about it, but I'm sure he'd have seen it behind the counter if you left it."

She watched as Lucy picked up a napkin, folded it into fourths, then absentmindedly dropped it on the table.

"Is it your aunt?" Dakota tried again.

Lucy looked down at her plastic tray. "You know, it's a sad state of affairs when school cafeteria food looks better than what you get at your own house."

"You didn't answer my question."

"Okay," Lucy sighed. "She caught me by surprise. Even though I should know better by now."

"I can't believe it either. I mean, what kind of mother takes off like that when her daughter's still missing?"

"Dr. Fielding advised her to go. He said it would be therapeutic. He said she couldn't do anything here anyway, except worry and be constantly reminded that Angela's gone. And she can stay in touch with the private investigator anywhere."

"Still . . . I think it's sad. It's like she's already decided that Angela's not coming home."

"It's so dark here . . . I can't get back . . ."

Remembering the ghostly telephone call, Lucy's shoulders stiffened. "Maybe she *has* to decide that. Maybe it's the only way she can cope."

"Maybe." Dakota gave a reluctant nod. "But it

sort of makes you understand why Angela's run away so many times, doesn't it?"

But this is the last time. The thought loomed darkly in Lucy's mind, though she tried to push it away. *This is the last time Angela will ever leave . . .*

"Lucy, I'll be leaving for a while. On very important business."

Irene's announcement had come that morning while she was driving Lucy to school. An announcement that was so casual and matter of fact, that at first Lucy hadn't even realized its magnitude.

"We're experiencing some difficulties with one of our foreign-exchange programs. It's necessary that I go to Paris and help with the reorganization."

Lucy had waited, not exactly sure what was coming next. Irene had cast her a pensive sidelong glance.

"It's going to take at least two weeks. Perhaps more. And frankly, I'm not sure what to do with you."

That's when the reality of the situation had

begun to sink in. And though Lucy felt stunned and hurt, she'd managed to shrug it off with a forced smile.

"You don't have to worry about me, Aunt Irene. I'll be fine."

"There's really no one I can think of to leave you with," her aunt had gone on, as though she found this mildly annoying. "And Florence can't be here full-time; she has a family and other clients to take care of."

"You don't have to ask Florence. It's not like I need a babysitter or anything."

A slight frown had settled between Irene's brows. "If you were Angela, I'd have to nag you about being responsible. I'd have to warn you not to let strangers into the house and not to throw wild parties while I was gone."

Lucy hadn't answered. She hadn't known what to say.

"But you're not Angela," Irene had concluded.

A pause had settled between them. And to Lucy's astonishment, Irene's eyes had suddenly glimmered with tears.

"And it's not your fault, Lucy," she'd said softly. "What happened is not your fault. I do not want you blaming yourself for any of Angela's rash behavior."

For one split second, Lucy had almost leaned toward her aunt. Almost touched her. Almost given her a hug.

But then the tears had vanished, leaving Irene's eyes as cold and hard as before.

"She'll come home. Eventually." As the car pulled up in front of the school, Irene's tone had suddenly matched her eyes. "When he breaks her heart . . . when she runs out of money. She'll come home like all the times before."

"Aunt Irene—"

"Don't be late, Lucy."

Crestfallen, Lucy had gotten out of the car.

She'd stood there on the sidewalk, and she'd even waved good-bye.

But Irene had never looked back . . .

". . . till she gets back," Dakota was saying.

Lucy looked up from her lumpy macaroni and cheese. The noise in the cafeteria was deafening, and she hadn't realized till this very minute how much her head was beginning to ache.

"Till *who* gets back?" she asked.

Dakota stopped sucking on her orange. She ran one hand slowly through her hair, her eyes fixed calmly on Lucy's face. "We were talking about your aunt."

"Sorry. I guess I zoned out for a minute."

"Oh, that's good. I thought maybe it was me zoning." Dakota slid her tray to the edge of the table. "I was just saying that you could stay with me while your aunt's gone. My parents would be totally okay with it."

"I couldn't do that. It's really nice of you, and I appreciate it, but . . ."

"But what?"

"But I just couldn't, that's all."

After a second's hesitation, Dakota reached over and squeezed Lucy's hand. "I don't know everything you've been through, Lucy. And I know this is none of my business. But I don't think you should be alone right now. So promise me you'll at least think about staying over."

"Yes." Lucy forced a weak smile. "I promise."

"When's she leaving, anyway?"

"Next week sometime."

"Well, you'd definitely start *eating* at my house," Dakota informed her. "My mom and dad are both great cooks. And I bet you'd sleep, too."

"I sleep now."

But Dakota wasn't fooled. Releasing Lucy's hand, she leaned even closer, a wise sadness in her eyes. "Be honest with me, Lucy—when's the last time you *really* slept? A sleep without nightmares . . . a sleep without pain?"

And Lucy couldn't answer.

Because she truly couldn't remember . . .

She'd stayed awake till morning.

Still restless from her need to be outside, Lucy had paced her bedroom in the dark, and she'd stared out for hours through the sliding glass doors. She'd sat on the bed with her arms wrapped around her, trying to give herself comfort. And she'd rocked back and forth, back and forth, but it hadn't lulled her to sleep.

As if she hadn't had enough on her mind already.

After Matt brought her home, she'd had more than enough to think about, a whole new set of fears to consider. She'd felt numb and strangely distant, as though her emotions belonged to someone else. For a while she'd held the medallion Matt had given her, turning it over and over in her hands. Then she'd put it in the drawer of the nightstand and collapsed on her bed, shutting her eyes and trying desperately to shut out the rest of the world.

A world she no longer trusted or understood.

A world of questions without answers.

The message in her notebook . . . Byron's face at the bookstore window . . . a series of wrong turns leading her straight to the Wetherly house . . .

And Byron's grandmother . . . Byron's reflection in those sad, dark eyes . . .

How did she know my name?

Lucy had lain there, too exhausted to move, and praying for sleep. Deep, senseless, peaceful sleep. Kind sleep . . . sleep without dreams.

But of course she hadn't slept.

Not then.

Not while those questions and conjectures had continued to rush blackly through her mind, like bats swarming at dusk from their cave.

Byron must have mentioned her, she'd decided.

At some point, Byron must have mentioned Lucy's name to his grandmother—or described her, maybe—and that's how his grandmother had known.

Yet how could Lucy explain the rest of it? Like her tire going flat, so conveniently near Byron's house? And Byron's grandmother recognizing her from countless other blond-haired, blue-eyed girls who might have happened to knock on her door?

"Mrs. Wetherly was propped up in bed, almost as if she'd been waiting for us. She didn't even look surprised. Just so sad . . . calm . . . resigned, almost."

Matt's words had come back to her then.

Matt's account of the night Byron died— when Matt and Father Paul and the sheriff and doctor had all gone to tell Byron's grandmother the news.

Could it be true?

Yielding reluctantly to her memories, Lucy had opened her eyes and stared hard at the ceiling. Byron had told her once that his grandmother had psychic powers, the ability to "know" things other people weren't privy to. Could it be that Mrs.

Wetherly had *expected* Lucy to show up there?

Could it be that she led me there deliberately?

The idea had been too chilling to contemplate.

So Lucy had gone into the bathroom and run a hot shower. She'd stood there under the steamy spray, but her mind had continued to fret.

Should I go back to Byron's house? Tell his grandmother how much he helped me, how much he meant to me?

Or should I stay away from there forever?

And even beneath the soothing flow of the water, Lucy had felt bruised and battered by indecision.

How much does Byron's grandmother know about me? How much did Byron tell her? Does she know about Katherine's horrible death? And how I found Katherine that night in the cemetery, and how Katherine changed me forever?

Lucy had leaned her head against the shower wall, picturing Byron's house again. The second-floor windows had been dark, she remembered. Windows where Katherine had stared out at an unsympathetic world . . . windows that had become Katherine's prison.

223

And suddenly her heart had ached for Katherine.

Ached and cried for Katherine.

Not only for the girl's heartless death, but for the life she'd been denied. Denied because of her powers. Denied because of her gift.

"A gift sometimes . . . but also a curse," Byron *had called it.*

And now it belonged to Lucy.

And as the shower washed away her tears, she'd wondered about her own life and the strange direction it had taken.

And she'd asked herself—as Dakota had asked her in the bookstore that night—just what *did* she believe in?

"Hope," said Dakota, and once again Lucy looked at her friend in total bewilderment.

"What?" Lucy asked.

"The candlelight vigil. As an expression of hope." Dakota was standing up now, closing her knapsack with a tolerant smile. "Lucy, I'll be glad to go over all this again when you're back on the planet."

"I'm sorry. I'm just so out of it today."

"Candlelight vigil," Dakota repeated patiently. "For Angela. Tomorrow night in front of the school."

"Whose idea was this?"

"Some of her friends on the cheerleading squad. At least that's what I heard."

"Does my aunt know about it?"

"I'm sure someone plans on telling her. Do you think she'll come?"

Lucy shrugged. "I've given up thinking what she might or might not do."

The two headed off to class. They were just rounding a corner near the office when Lucy spotted several of the cheerleaders standing together, handing out flyers.

"Those are the notices," Dakota mumbled. "For the vigil tomorrow night."

As they got nearer, Lucy's heart began to quicken. She recognized one of the girls as Wanda Carver, and she stopped uncertainly in the middle of the hall.

"What?" Dakota stopped, too, her expression puzzled. "What is it?"

"Nothing. I'm okay."

"You sure?"

Lucy nodded. But her heart was beating faster now, and she could see Wanda starting toward her, one hand extended, passing Lucy one of the printed announcements.

Lucy stood frozen. Wanda was looking at her strangely, as strangely as Dakota was, and Lucy couldn't move, couldn't move even though she wanted to, even though she wanted to turn and run and never touch that paper that Wanda was touching . . .

But Wanda thrust the flyer into her hand, and Lucy had to take it. Had to take it and pretend nothing was wrong, while the quick, sharp flashes of danger strobed darkly through her brain.

"Lucy? You did this last time—what's wrong?"

And she could hear Dakota's voice so close to her as she whirled around and started away, away from the curious stares and away from the feeling of tragedy . . .

She's going to die on Thursday.

"I have to go back," Lucy said.

Breaking from Dakota's grasp, she pushed her way through the packed corridor. Wanda didn't even see her coming, not till Lucy was right beside her and leaning in close to her ear.

"Be careful," Lucy whispered. "Be careful tomorrow. Please."

The girl jumped back, completely startled and completely annoyed. "Hey, what do you think you are doing?"

"You could get hurt. You could fall and get hurt. Just please be careful."

"Get away from me! Are you *crazy*?"

Lucy pulled back. Wanda and her friends were staring at her with undisguised contempt, and Lucy's cheeks flamed in embarrassment.

"Sorry," she mumbled. "I just . . . It's a mistake. Sorry."

Turning on her heel, she ran to catch up with Dakota. But her heart was still pounding.

And the images in her mind had gone hopelessly black.

23

She and Dakota had almost been late for class.

Which is a good thing, Lucy reminded herself wryly.

There'd been no time for Dakota to question Lucy's strange behavior, no time for Wanda Carver to mortify Lucy more than she already had.

Still, by the end of the day, Lucy couldn't help noticing more curious stares and secretive whispers aimed in her general direction.

Lucy Dennison. Certified Nut Case.

She wished she could just go straight home and hide, but she'd already had to beg a ride from Dakota. Angela's car was waiting at Glen's Repair, and after that, Irene had asked her to pick up some dry cleaning.

"We can do that first," Dakota offered, coaxing

her truck from the school parking lot. "It's right next to the soup kitchen where I volunteer."

Lucy was impressed. "Do you really? I've always wanted to do that. What's it like?"

"Interesting. And humbling. It definitely keeps me grounded."

"Do you feed a big crowd?"

"Not like a lot of places, thank goodness." Dakota raised an eyebrow. "Pine Ridge is pretty affluent. But we have our share of homeless. You get to know the regulars. And then there're the ones just passing through town."

"So when do you work?"

"Saturdays mostly. But around holidays or when it's really cold, I work during the week, too."

"Do you think I could help out sometime?"

Looking genuinely pleased, Dakota nodded. "We'd love to have you. Would you like to stop by now and see it for yourself?"

"That'd be great."

As Dakota continued to drive, Lucy lapsed into silence. Several minutes passed before she cast her friend a troubled look.

"Dakota, I need a job."

She'd halfway expected shock at this announcement. At the very least, reminders about her aunt being one of the richest people in Pine Ridge. Dakota, however, kept her eyes on the road and creased her brow in thought.

"Doing what?" she asked.

"I don't know. Something useful." Shifting in the seat, she gave her friend a hard stare. "The thing is, Irene keeps telling me to use her credit cards. I don't want to ask her for anything. But there's stuff I need. And I don't have any money of my own."

Dakota's voice was quiet. "I understand."

"So do you know of anything?"

"Well . . . shops around here always need part-time help around Christmas. But they usually snap up the college kids first." She paused, fingers tightening on the steering wheel. "My dad might know of something. And I'll ask around, too. There's bound to be someone out there who needs you."

"You mean, they're just waiting for me to come along and walk right through their door?" Lucy couldn't help teasing.

"That's exactly what I mean."

The smile faded from Lucy's face. "You're really serious."

"Of course I am. You should know that by now."

"So you *really* believe that somebody who needs *one* particular job done is waiting *just* for me—out of *all* the other people in the universe."

Dakota's glance was solemn. "Lucy," she said, "there are no coincidences."

Lucy frowned, a sliver of uneasiness shinnying up her spine. Dakota's eyes shifted back to the windshield and stayed there the rest of the way. When they finally pulled up in front of the dry cleaner's, Lucy grabbed Dakota's arm before the girl could get out of the truck.

"Aren't you going to ask me?" she demanded.

Dakota gazed back at her, those pale blue eyes calm on Lucy's face.

"Ask you what?" Dakota murmured.

"You know. About Wanda Carver. About those weird spells I have. About what happened today."

"Do you want me to?" Dakota countered softly.

"Well, don't you think I'm crazy like everybody else does?"

That hint of a smile drifted over Dakota's mouth. She rested her hand on Lucy's.

"You're not crazy. You're a person with many secrets. And secrets should never be told until their time. And when they're ready to be told, then you'll tell me."

Lucy didn't know whether to laugh or to cry.

"Come on," Dakota said, shoving open the door. "Let's go sign you up."

Lucy instantly felt at home.

As Dakota showed her around the soup kitchen and introduced her to the staff, Lucy knew she'd made the right decision about volunteering. She hadn't felt such a warm, welcoming atmosphere since moving to Pine Ridge.

Not since her mother had died.

"See?" Dakota looked almost smug as she guided Lucy through the oversized pantry. "These are wonderful people. You fit right in."

"Thanks for letting me join."

"No. Thank *you*." Taking Lucy's arm, Dakota

led her to the main dining area. "Come on. I'll show you how we do the serving line. Just think of it as your friendly neighborhood buffet."

The room was practically empty. Three elderly women in threadbare coats sat at a table in one corner, chuckling over some shared bit of gossip, their raggedy shopping bags beside them on the floor. They waved to Dakota as she passed them, then went on with their conversation. Behind the serving counter, Dakota pointed out the contents of shelves and explained portion sizes, while Lucy listened attentively. She scarcely even noticed when the front door opened and the disheveled figure slunk in.

"Okay, here's someone," Dakota murmured, glancing toward the approaching stranger. "Perfect time to practice."

"Now?" Lucy asked hesitantly.

"Of course, now. Here. Just do it like I showed you."

Nodding, Lucy picked up a ladle and waited for the man to take a bowl. Dakota walked to the end of the counter where a few pieces of chocolate cake still remained in their baking pan.

"Hi," Lucy smiled, as the man stopped in front of the huge soup kettle.

For a moment he paused there, head lowered.

And then he looked up at her.

Dear God . . .

Lucy's fingers dug into the ladle, the smile frozen on her lips. For one panicky second she wondered if she'd actually been able to keep her face expressionless, if she'd managed to keep the revulsion from showing in her eyes.

His cheeks were scarred, this man standing before her—scarred and festering with sores. Across his forehead and through the matted beard on his chin, Lucy could see pus oozing out beneath big, wet scabs. Long hair lay over his shoulders in greasy strands. His body was rail-thin, his weary shoulders slumped, and the odor emanating from his tattered clothes made the bile rise into Lucy's throat.

She hastily tried to collect herself.

But she couldn't look away from his eyes.

His eyes . . .

At first glance she'd guessed him to be

young—somewhere in his twenties, perhaps. And yet his eyes were old.

The eyes of a very old man.

Eyes of vast experience. Intelligence and cunning.

Tragedy . . . but survival.

And as Lucy peered into their rheumy depths, she felt an unnerving shiver pass through her.

"Hi," she heard herself mumble again.

Beneath his coarse mustache, she thought he might have smiled. Rotten teeth and foul breath.

His eyes flickered dimly . . . some emotion she couldn't read.

Lucy plunged the ladle into the pot. Her hand was trembling, and she glanced up to see the man still watching her.

His hand was trembling like her own.

Trembling as he held out his empty bowl, waiting for her to fill it.

A rush of pity went through her. Pity and an understanding of his soul.

On his face . . . in his eyes . . . through the quivering of his hand, Lucy recognized the depth of isolation. The aching loneliness and despair. The qualities that kept him distant and apart.

Before she even realized what she was doing, she'd reached across the counter, taken his bowl, and in its place, laid her hand in his.

"I'm so glad you came today," she said softly.

He gazed at her in silence.

A penetrating silence as he slowly squeezed her hand.

Lucy's breath caught in her throat. For the space of one heartbeat, the air seemed to swell and split around her, as though something in the very atmosphere had changed.

Her head grew light.

Her skin flushed warm.

And from some very distant place came the burning familiarity of a deep, insistent ache . . .

"Lucy?"

Startled, Lucy turned toward the sound of a voice.

Dakota was standing beside her, easing the ladle from Lucy's clamped fingers.

"I think you've stirred that soup long enough," Dakota teased. "Save some of your strength for next time."

Lucy's eyes quickly scanned the room. Except for the three women still talking in their corner, all the tables were empty.

"Where'd he go?" Lucy asked.

"Who?"

"The man who came in to eat."

"He left about fifteen minutes ago." Dakota gave her a funny look. "Didn't you notice?"

"I . . . I guess not."

"Now, that's what I call being involved in your work." As Lucy stared down at the counter, Dakota stepped back, studying her with a thoughtful frown. "But you're upset, aren't you? About that man."

Lucy didn't answer. Her hands felt cold now, her mind hazy—as though she'd just awakened from a dream.

"I know how you feel," Dakota said, trying to comfort her. "It was hard for me, too, at first. Seeing people like that, and wanting so much to help them. But we *are* helping. Just for the time they're here, we *are* making a difference in their lives."

"Who was he?" Lucy's voice was tight. "Do you know?"

"That's odd, isn't it? He must be one of those transients I was telling you about. I've never seen him around here before."

With a sigh, Dakota gazed out the front window, out at the people and shadows mingling together in the dusk.

"You were so kind to him, Lucy. He'll probably never forget you."

24

Her touch still clung to him.

He could still feel the pressure of her hand in his . . . the softness of her skin . . . the length and slender shape of every finger.

Her warmth had flowed into him, a surge of emotions that had shocked each one of his senses into wonder.

Her concern and compassion . . . her undisguised pity . . .

And the sorrowful understanding in her eyes.

It had left him stunned and seriously shaken, a wound within the nether regions of his soul, for seldom in his lifetime had he ever known understanding.

Understanding made one vulnerable.

A lesson he'd learned well, and long ago.

So now he paced, gripped by a strange,

trembling restlessness, his skin too tight, his face transforming into another. He paced like an animal in a cage, stopping only long enough to gaze out through the darkness—the deep, deceptive darkness that was his only friend.

This was his domain, as it had always been, as it would always be.

This kingdom of the night, as black and impenetrable as his soul.

"Damn her."

How could his plan have gone so completely awry?

"*Damn her!*"

What had he expected? Another ruse to get close to her, to hide behind the essence of his nature and see himself reflected in her eyes.

And for a single moment, he had watched her hovering there on the brink of disgust and aversion, startled by his ugliness and trying not to show it, drowning in the poison of his stare.

But then, without warning, she'd changed.

He had not expected it—not even seen it coming—when suddenly he'd *felt* it. *Felt* it like warm, soothing waves; like gentle arms reaching out to take him in, into a place of comfort and acceptance. He felt it a thousand times stronger than *anything* he'd felt from her before.

He had been so fascinated, so dismayed, he'd simply stood frozen there in place and squeezed her hand.

It had been all he could do not to moan out loud.

Moan with the desire for her, the *need* for her, the wild and desperate hunger for her.

For he had felt *her* longing, as well.

Her ache as strong as his, as deep and unfulfilled, the frantic throbbing of her pulse, and their connection so strong, so overwhelming, it had sucked his breath away . . .

Distracted his instincts . . . driven him mad.

Since he'd left the soup kitchen, he'd thought of nothing else.

He had no choice but to go to her.

Force her if he had to, take her *now* if he had to—he would *not* wait for willingness or surrender or the right and perfect time.

But even as he crouched upon her balcony, where he'd spent so many nights before, he knew that he must hold himself in check. Remain anonymous and watchful. Infinitely patient. Disguised as whomever she needed him to be.

Like fine gray mist, he slipped inside her room.

Gazed upon her silently as she slept.

Damn her for making him feel!

For touching him like that . . . with her hand and with her heart!

For making him remember another life in another time, times of understanding . . . times of sharing love . . .

No, he would *not* feel—he would *not* remember!

He would feed.

And he would kill.

And he would survive.

For these were the only things that mattered to him now.

The only things he loved and understood.

25

Lucy still couldn't understand what had happened.

Everything had been so normal, everything had been going so well—spending the afternoon with Dakota, and meeting the people at the soup kitchen, and volunteering for something that really mattered.

And then that stranger had come in.

That pathetic young man with the festering sores and the hunger in his very old eyes.

She hadn't been able to stop herself.

She'd reached out her hand and she'd touched him, and slowly she'd begun to recognize something.

Something that had touched her before.

Impossible.

Absolutely impossible.

But now she was lying in bed and thinking back on the whole unsettling experience, trying to tell herself it was only one of those blackouts Dr. Fielding had warned her about, one of those memory lapses.

After all . . . hadn't she lost fifteen whole minutes?

Fifteen minutes unaccounted for, while the stranger had sat down at a table and eaten his meal and left again by the front door?

Of course it had been just memory loss.

How else could she ever explain it?

Yet a doubt still persisted in the back of her mind . . . a nagging doubt and a lingering nightmare . . .

A nightmare swift and needle-sharp—stabbing like fire, piercing hot through my skin, sinking deep through my flesh, clamping down and holding on, suspended there . . .

Lucy turned restlessly, unable to sleep.

Shadows pressed around the bed and shrouded her in black.

Suspended there on boiling waves of panic and burning pleasure . . .

The room seemed to be holding its breath as her fingertips stroked the darkness.

Burning pleasure . . . waves rushing over me . . . through me . . .

Once again Lucy pictured the stranger's face.

She pulled the covers over her head and hid beneath them till morning.

26

He had felt her fingertips caressing his cheek . . . gliding over his throat . . . down the front of his chest.

She hadn't even known what she'd done.

Hadn't even realized how close he'd been standing, only inches away from her bed.

But now it was one stroke past midnight.

He'd been watching the hands of the clock on her nightstand, the minutes creeping by like hours, the hours stretching out like the endless decades of his life.

Lucy's restlessness was nothing, compared to his own.

His growing frustration, his need to be filled.

There was only one thing that could satisfy him.

And he would be no gentleman tonight.

He ran through the woods and on through the town, his midnight senses keen and alert, the darkness flowing over him like wind.

It was in the park where he finally caught the girl's scent.

Not virginal blood, but deliciously seasoned all the same.

She was small and well built, athletic and strong, with very short hair, like a boy's. She had books under one arm and she smelled of sweet powder, strained peaches, and soft, fluffy blankets.

She had been babysitting.

And now she was on her way home.

He trailed her over a footbridge, then slunk out of sight behind the trees and the bushes, just one more shadow among many. He kept pace with her and wondered how long it would be until she sensed she was being followed.

Not so long, after all.

Like countless times before, he recognized that first dawning hint of awareness, that first wary glance back over the shoulder, that first startled quickening of the feet.

He always enjoyed that initial shock. That

primal instinct of approaching death, innate to every species.

For a while she walked faster, and so did he.

Then suddenly she stopped and turned to face him.

"Who's there?" she called in a quivering voice, trying so hard to be brave. "I know you're there; you're not scaring me."

And so he let her see him.

He watched her eyes go wide; he smelled her helpless terror. The thrill of the hunt surged through him—that heady anticipation of the kill, that stamina and speed no mortal could ever hope to match.

Just for fun, he gave her a head start.

She screamed, but no one heard.

And for one desperate minute of her tragically young life, he let her think she might actually get away.

But he had no patience for the chase tonight.

And he was upon her so quickly, she didn't even struggle.

Afterward he lay there on the cold, wet ground, feeling empty and disappointed . . . gorged but unfulfilled.

The dead girl's eyes stared up at him. There was no malice there, no accusation—but rather a look of blank and sad surprise.

He took her to the footbridge that spanned the concrete drainage ditch.

With one swift motion he broke her neck for good measure, then tossed her over the railing.

New power for every life . . .

A new century for every soul.

With a bitter smile, he went back into the night . . . as silently and stealthily as he had come.

27

"You can't do this, Matt," Lucy said. "There's got to be another way. You *can't* just put her in some nursing home."

Startled, Matt glanced up from his desk. Lucy was standing rigidly in the doorway of the office, looking close to tears.

"Do we have an appointment?" Hurriedly he pretended to search through his calendar. Lucy was not amused.

"Matt, this is serious. How could you do such a terrible thing?"

"Lucy, *I'm* not doing it. And who told *you* about it?"

"Dakota heard some people talking in the bookstore last night. Some of Byron's neighbors, I guess."

Matt leaned back in his chair. He steepled his fingers beneath his chin and slowly shook his head.

"Mrs. Dempsey can't stay forever, and we can't expect her to. It was always understood that the arrangement was temporary."

"Yes," Lucy reminded him. "Till you could find someone else. But you *haven't* found anyone else yet."

"And it doesn't look like we're going to. Look, I'm as sorry about it as you are, Lucy, but we don't have a choice. Even with the nurse and with neighbors being kind enough to drop in, Byron's grandmother can't be alone at night."

"Then I'll do it."

Lifting an eyebrow, Matt stared at her. "What do you mean, you'll do it?"

"My aunt's going on a trip to Paris. She'll be gone at least two weeks and—"

"The woman's compassion knows no bounds," he groaned. "Are you serious?"

"She told me yesterday. Some sort of exchange program at the university. And I really don't want to stay in that house by myself."

"Well, you *shouldn't*. I'm really sorry, Lucy—"

"The thing is," Lucy interrupted, not feeling up to sympathy at the moment, "do you think Byron's grandmother would even *want* me there?"

"Why wouldn't she?"

"You know why. Maybe she couldn't even stand to look at me. And I wouldn't blame her."

"She's not like that. She's very sweet. Even Mrs. Dempsey says so." Folding his arms behind his head, Matt leaned back even farther. "And if anyone can manage to stay sweet around Mrs. Dempsey, they qualify for sainthood in my opinion."

"Can you arrange it?" Lucy pleaded, but Matt hedged.

"Lucy . . . are you sure you want to do this for the right reasons?"

"I have good reasons."

"Yeah, but . . . maybe you're thinking more about how bad *you* feel, than about how bad *Mrs. Wetherly* feels." Pausing, he added, "It won't work as penance, you know."

Lucy's voice lowered. "But won't my being there help *both* of us?"

For a long moment Matt said nothing. Then finally he gave a deep sigh.

"And I suppose you want me to talk to your aunt about it, too?"

"Would you? If anyone can convince her, you can."

"Thanks. I think." Matt's smile was dubious. "There's the bell. You better get to class."

But Lucy didn't move. "Are you going to the vigil tonight?"

"Actually, I've been asked to say a few words. What about you?"

"I'm coming with Irene."

There was another lengthy hesitation before he spoke. "You think you're up to this?"

"Do I really have a choice?"

With a grim expression she turned to leave, then promptly faced him again.

"Matt?"

"Yes?"

"That medallion you gave me? You never told me anything about—"

"Bell." He pointed sternly toward the hallway. "Late. Go."

Lucy made it to homeroom just in time. Sliding into her seat, she rested one cheek on her pile of books and gazed out the window as the morning's announcements came over the intercom.

In the distance she could see a large group heading off toward the athletic field—coaches, cheerleaders, band members, even some football players, it looked like. And though they were too far away to distinguish each face individually, it was obvious they were all in high spirits—laughing, jostling, joking around.

Lucy's heart melted in relief.

Everyone was happy. Everything was fine. It was Thursday and no one had died . . .

"And no one's *going* to die. And whatever I saw in my mind was a *mistake*. And I'm *not* turning into Katherine."

But she realized she was whispering to herself, and that her hands were clamped tightly over her ears, trying to drown out *another* voice—a sad, empty voice whispering far back in the darkness of her mind . . .

Everything's not *fine, Lucy . . .*

And it's only morning.

The candlelight vigil was scheduled for seven-thirty.

As Lucy let herself into the house that afternoon, it was obvious Irene wasn't there yet. No messages on the answering machine. No notes beside the phone.

She hoped Irene remembered.

How would it look if Angela's own mother didn't attend the service?

Lucy wished she could miss it herself. She dreaded the emotional impact of the ceremony—it had been looming over her like a dark cloud all day. Now she just wanted to get it over with.

Peeling off her coat and gloves, she threw them over the bannister and went up to her room. She was dressed and ready by six o'clock. Dressed for the weather and feeling edgy because Irene still wasn't home.

Darkness had already fallen, and as lights began coming on throughout the house, Lucy went downstairs to turn on more.

By seven, she was really getting worried. Pacing around the kitchen, she nearly jumped out of her skin when the telephone rang. She hesitated, suddenly afraid to pick it up, then heard Irene's voice on the machine.

"Lucy, are you there? I'm running late. Just go on without me, and I'll meet you at the school."

Relieved, Lucy started back to her room to grab another sweater.

But the doorbell stopped her halfway.

She hurried down again, then looked nervously out through the peephole. Within the distorted angle of the lens, she could see a tall figure standing on the porch, his back to her, a clipboard dangling from one hand.

Cautiously, Lucy cracked open the front door.

"Special delivery," the man announced. But he didn't turn around, and Lucy stood there on the threshold, watching him in wary surprise.

"It's kind of late," she said. "What kind of delivery?"

"Are you Lucy Dennison?"

Hesitating, Lucy nodded. "Yes, that's me."

"Then sign here."

She saw him turn around. Saw his pale sharp features and his deep-set eyes as he fixed her with a steady gaze. Both his truck and his uniform were black, but neither of them were printed with a name.

"What is it?" Lucy's voice tightened. "Who's it from?"

His gaze lingered a moment longer. "Well," he said at last, "I imagine that's part of the surprise." He thrust a clipboard at her. It had a pen attached to it, and a sheet of paper that was blank. "Just sign your name. I have other appointments to keep."

Again Lucy hesitated. Then she quickly scribbled her name.

"But what delivery company are you with?" she persisted.

"I told you. A special one."

Before she could ask anything more, the man turned and walked off. Lucy watched him climb into his truck and drive away from the house.

Then she looked down at the box.

It was fairly large—and seemed to weigh a ton. When Lucy couldn't lift it, she finally managed to drag it into the hall, then locked the door and stood there, frowning down at the package.

Who would be sending her a special delivery? And why?

She chewed anxiously on a fingernail. She

stood and tapped her foot, trying to decide what to do.

She didn't have time for packages right now; she had to get to the vigil. She had to meet Irene. She had to be brave and strong.

She glanced at her watch.

If she hurried, she'd still have time to open the box. It wouldn't take that long to drive over to the high school, and since this thing was a special delivery, then it must be something important.

Yet still she stood and stared at it.

Watching as if something might suddenly unwrap itself and jump out at her.

She was being silly—paranoid—but her curiosity was stronger.

Retrieving some scissors from the kitchen, she cut away the mailing tape and lifted the cardboard flaps on top.

It was wrapped very tight, very thickly.

Whatever it was, it had been well protected and packed with great care.

Lucy got a knife from the kitchen drawer. With painstaking caution, she began to work the heavy padding loose.

She was almost there.

She could feel something beneath the filling now . . . something hard and heavy and cold and smooth . . .

No, not quite smooth . . .

Mostly smooth, but with something carved into its surface.

Words? Numbers?

With one final tug, the packing material came away in her hands. Lucy leaned forward into the light and gazed down into the box.

Oh God . . . Oh God, no . . .

The headstone was gray, crowned with a gently rounded arch.

And its design was stark and simple, except for the large black letters engraved deeply across the front.

ANGELA FOSTER

RIP

28

She thought she might have screamed.

Stumbling backward, Lucy heard a distant, anguished cry, the strangled voice of someone she barely even recognized.

She groped for the wall, for something—*anything*—to hold on to. Yet her eyes remained fixed on the headstone and the name that would be on everyone's minds, on everyone's lips, in less than fifteen minutes.

Her knees gave way.

She crumpled on to the floor.

Burying her face in her hands, she tried to think what to do, but her mind wouldn't cooperate. *Call the police? Get out of the house? Go to someone for help?*

Matt would be at the vigil by now. Dakota,

too. Thank God, Irene hadn't come home tonight.

Irene . . .

Lucy's hands slid away from her eyes.

She had to hide the headstone from Irene. No matter what course of action she ultimately decided to take, she couldn't leave the headstone here for Irene to see. She'd have to put it somewhere else. She'd have to *hide* it somewhere else. At least for the time being.

The vigil was just about ready to start. She was already late, and everyone was sure to notice if she didn't show up. There was no way she'd ever lift that box. Maybe she could get Dakota or Matt to help her later, but for now she'd have to hide it somewhere close. Somewhere close enough to drag it.

Frantically she looked around the downstairs. She couldn't focus, couldn't concentrate. *Call the police—I have to call the police! This time I have something* real *to show them—this time they'll have to believe me!*

But she couldn't call them right now, she couldn't tell them about the deliveryman and the unmarked truck and this horrible, hideous headstone; she had to get to the service for Angela.

Another sick joke?

If it was, someone had gone to an awful lot of trouble and expense just to pull it off. They'd have had to be sure it was delivered here just in time. They'd have had to be sure Lucy was home to receive it.

Would kids at school go to all that effort?

And if they *had* done it, would they be at the vigil tonight, waiting to see her reaction?

But she didn't have time to go over that now. She had to get rid of the headstone.

She could feel her thoughts jumping back and forth, exploding like firecrackers. No matter where she hid the headstone, Irene would be sure to find it. And if Irene didn't, then Florence *certainly* would—the woman was fastidious about cleaning every nook and cranny of this house.

So I can't hide it in here. I'll have to put it outside.

Her watch read seven-thirty now. Irene would be at the vigil, wondering where she was—and Lucy had no idea what she'd tell her.

I'll think of something—I'll worry about that later.

With all the force she could muster, Lucy began dragging the box toward the front door. If she could just get it out on the porch, she might be able to tip it off into the shrubbery. At least the front of the house was landscaped with evergreens—if she worked it underneath some of the branches and piled dead leaves over it, no one was likely to spot it, even if they stood right there and rang the bell.

At least it's worth a try.

At least till Irene's away from the house, so I can report it to the police.

Or at least till I can come up with a better idea . . .

Later she wondered if fear and shock had given her superhuman strength—but for now, all Lucy cared about was wrestling that carton underneath the bushes. As it landed with a dull thud, she hastily camouflaged it, then hurried to the car and drove straight to Pine Ridge High.

She didn't even remember the ride over.

It was as if her mind had detached from the rest of her, and stayed behind with Angela's headstone. She didn't know how she was going to face Irene, knowing what she knew, knowing what she'd just hidden beside the porch. How would she ever be able to act normally? Act as if nothing were wrong?

"But everything's wrong," Lucy whispered.

The sound of her own voice startled her.

Slowly, she began to come back to herself, and she realized she was parked at the school. She could see a huge circle of glowing light on the front lawn of the campus—dozens of tiny, flickering candle flames, and the shadowy figures of those who held them.

Voices were singing softly. Some popular song she felt she should recognize, but couldn't.

Go on. You have to.

Yet still she sat there, watching from a distance. Thinking about the headstone. Wondering what it meant.

She hadn't wanted to admit that Angela might never come home again, even though at times she'd felt it so strongly.

And now . . .

It doesn't mean anything!

Lucy shook her head, fighting back angry

tears. Angela had run away, just like all those times before, and Angela would come home again, just like Irene had predicted.

Lucy wanted to believe that.

Even now . . . she still wanted *so much* to believe that.

Taking in a deep gulp of air, Lucy willed herself to get out of the car. She stood for a moment, trying to empty her mind of bad thoughts, trying to compose her features into some semblance of hope.

She started walking toward the light.

And even before she got there, she sensed that something was wrong.

At first it was the subtle shifting of the crowd . . . the murmurs of curiosity and confusion . . . the gradual fading of voices, one by one.

Uneasy glances and eyes going wide . . .

Then cries of shock and disbelief.

As Lucy approached the circle, the first one she spotted was Matt.

He looked stunned and speechless, and all around him people had frozen in place like statues.

Irene was standing rigidly beside him. Her expression seemed to be caught somewhere between sheer relief and sheer horror.

Above each fluttering candle flame, faces had turned to stiff and bloodless masks.

Lucy saw the police.

She saw Dakota breaking through the circle, pushing her way slowly over to where Lucy had stopped to stare.

She felt her own lips move, though no sound came out.

And she heard Dakota answer her directly, as if Lucy's silent question had been spoken all too clearly.

"It's Wanda Carver." Dakota's face was the color of ash. "They found her in the park tonight. Just about an hour ago."

The world began to shimmer.

The world and Dakota's face and the glowing circle of hope, all shimmering through the swell of Lucy's tears.

"She's dead," Lucy murmured.

Dakota nodded. "She fell off the footbridge over that old drainage ditch in the park. She broke her neck on the concrete."

"When . . . When did it happen?"

"They're saying it happened sometime early this morning." Dakota's gaze was calm and unwavering. "But then . . . you already knew that, didn't you?"

29

She hadn't been able to talk.

She hadn't been able to answer Dakota's quiet accusation, or to defend herself, or to think of anything else except getting out of there and getting away.

She'd turned and run.

Run to the car and driven off.

She'd driven with no idea of where to go or how to get there—simply driven all over town, up one street and down another, till she began to think that Irene might be wondering about her and that she'd probably better get back to the house.

It had actually surprised her to see Irene sitting up, waiting for her. The woman's face had been taut and bewildered, and she'd stared at Lucy for a long, long time, as though her niece were a total stranger.

"When they said they'd found a girl, I thought it was Angela." Irene had finally spoken, though her eyes had been fixed on a place far beyond Lucy. "And then it was someone else. And I was glad."

Irene's numb gaze had turned to Lucy then. And her voice had faltered.

"How cruel of me," she'd mumbled. "To be glad some other girl's dead."

Lucy had felt so helpless. She'd walked over to her aunt's chair, and she'd laid a hand on her aunt's stiff shoulder.

"Aunt Irene . . ."

"She'll be home," Irene had said softly. "It's just a matter of time, you'll see—and Angela will be home."

"Aunt Irene—"

"Go to bed now, Lucy."

But she couldn't stay in bed any longer.

Now Lucy got dressed and slipped quietly from the house. She backed the car down the driveway and headed for Pine Ridge Cemetery.

What little sleep she'd managed to get last night had been fraught with reality and tormented with the truth.

The truth she must finally face.

The truth she must finally accept.

It's real.

Lucy watched the cold, gray dawn creep slowly through the trees. A patina of frost coated the houses and lawns, and a lazy sun continued to slumber behind a thin layer of clouds.

The gift Katherine gave me . . . the powers Katherine gave me . . .

Real.

They're all real.

How could she have ignored it for so long? Been so unwilling to believe?

Because to believe in this gift means believing in other things, too. The dreams and the nightmares, the feelings and visions, the instincts I've never been able to trust before . . .

The existence of unbelievable things . . . un-explainable things . . .

Evil and unseen things.

She felt as if she'd betrayed herself.

And somehow . . . even worse . . . betrayed Byron.

Tears dampened her cheeks. Her heart ached with grief and regret.

When Byron was here, he'd shown her the truth. Shown her a destiny and purpose. Convinced her that her journey, no matter how dangerous or uncertain, was still necesssary and worthwhile.

She'd lost so much in the accident that night.

Byron.

Her faith . . .

Her self.

If only she could have them all back again.

If only she could speak to Byron one more time . . .

So that's why she'd decided to visit the cemetery this morning. To sit beside Byron's resting place and try to sort things out. She wanted to tell him everything, everything that had happened since he'd died. And she wanted to think that somehow he might really hear her . . . help her figure out what to do . . . help her make sense of things.

She wanted to believe that maybe—somehow—she wasn't really as alone as she felt.

But after entering the cemetery, Lucy began to have second thoughts. She hadn't expected it to look so spooky at this hour of the morning. Like wandering phantoms, tatters of soft white mist hovered among the graves, and an unnatural quiet smothered the sound of her footsteps as she made her way to the remote section of the burial grounds. The dead slept deep and undisturbed. Remembered and forgotten alike, they surrounded her on all sides, rotting peacefully to dust.

In the distance, the Wetherly mausoleum came darkly into view, silhouetted against the gloom. As Lucy got nearer, she could see the wrought-iron gates and stone angels that guarded it, and for one unsettling moment, she remembered her dream about Byron and his warning.

"Keep away . . . there's no one in this place."

An icy shudder worked its way up her spine. Hesitating, she dug her hands into her coat pockets and glanced back over her shoulder.

Come on, Lucy, get a grip.

It was easy to imagine eerie whispers and invisible watchers in a creepy place like this— what had she been thinking anyway, coming here so early?

Stop scaring yourself. Nobody here can hurt you.

Giving herself a stern mental shake, she walked over to the front of the tomb. To her surprise, the double gates weren't padlocked as she'd assumed they'd be—in fact, they were standing partway open, one of them creaking rustily as the breeze swung it back and forth.

Heart quickening, Lucy glanced around a second time.

If someone *were* here, they'd be impossible to see, she admitted to herself. Anyone could be hiding close by or far away.

Lucy suppressed another shiver.

Turning in a slow circle, she scanned the graves and headstones, the sepulchres and statues, the trees and shadows and mist. A taste of fear crept into her throat, and she tried to choke it down.

Cautiously, she turned back to the gates.

Taking one in each hand, she eased them open the rest of the way. Cracks had widened along the foundation, and leaves had sifted in over the broken, weathered stones of the floor.

Holding her breath, Lucy walked into the crypt.

She saw the muddy footprints and tufts of clotted hair; the dark, reddish-brown stains smeared along the walls . . .

But she didn't see the figure behind her.

Not till she turned and screamed and stumbled from his arms, trying wildly to fight her way free.

And then she stared up, shocked, into eyes as black and deep as midnight.

"Oh my God," she choked. "Who are you?"

The dark-haired young man gazed coolly back at her.

"Byron's brother," he answered. "Who the hell are *you*?"

TURN THE PAGE FOR A SNEAK PEEK AT THE NEXT CHILLING INSTALLMENT

The Unseen

part 3

blood brothers

Prologue

He'd had to think quickly.

After this last kill he'd been so gorged, so utterly exhausted from frenzy and frustration, he'd been unable to return to his bed. He'd been forced to seek out another hiding place . . . and then he'd crept inside and he'd slept.

Slept far past his normal hour of waking . . .

Slept right through the day . . . into the night . . .

Slept the fathomless sleep of the dead.

He'd never seen the attack coming.

Never awakened fully, even, until the first hot spurt of blood, the first scream of ripping flesh, the whole world exploding in a thick, wet fountain of scarlet and black.

He had no idea which of them had struck the

first blow. Or when instinct had taken ahold of him, every primal sense honed for survival, no matter what the pain, no matter what the cost . . .

He did not remember which had been the last to fall . . .

He was only and finally aware of the silence and the peace. The wind upon his face, the snow upon his lips. He was thirsty, yet could not seem to drink. He needed warmth and shelter, yet could not seem to move.

He was in desperate agony, yet could not help himself.

And so he lay there, stunned and weakened, too sick to lick his wounds. Until at last, and like a dream, the sound of quiet footsteps had floated through his mind . . .

He heard them from a distance, moving closer and closer, phantom footsteps of no real concern, no imminent danger. But as he struggled to comprehend them, he realized these footsteps were no dream at all.

They were real, and they were human.

They were coming toward the burial place, dangerously close to where he rested.

And so he'd had to think quickly.

Think quickly and act with haste.

Transform to a shadow? Mist? A guise of the living, a memory of the dead?

Or, in one swift, smooth motion, ready himself to strike again?

But then he paused, consumed by an ache so deep, he had not even realized he moaned.

For now he saw this was no enemy.

Now he realized this was Lucy—his Lucy—approaching him unaware and unsuspecting, steeped in grief and sorrow as he had always known her.

And yet . . . different somehow.

Unsettlingly different, somehow.

He could feel it, as sharply as he could feel the rats cowering around him, their ears twitching in fear, their glowing eyes averted from his own, their teeth stained red from the remnants of his meal and the raw meat of his wound. And he could smell it, too—as surely as he smelled the slow and steady creeping of decay, the lingering despair of so many wasted lives rotting in the graves around him.

No, Lucy was not quite the same as before.

Something had changed since he'd last laid eyes upon her.

Despite her confusion, there was now resolve.

And amid her fear and helplessness burned a new strength—small yet, to be sure, but solid with determination.

How interesting, he thought . . . and how curious.

And also how very delightful. So delightful, it made him smile, despite his anguish.

He couldn't help wondering what had happened—one incident? or many?—to touch her at such a profound level in so short a time.

But no matter.

This newfound strength of Lucy's would only serve to make the Game more interesting. More challenging. More worth the winning.

So he'd narrowed his eyes and waited.

Waited until her footsteps were practically upon him.

Until, in one more second, Lucy would be at the gates of the mausoleum, peering into the shadows of the tomb, stepping across that crumbling threshold between life and death.

Could he take her? As this desperate need for

her surged through every vein, filling him with brief and savage power?

Yes . . . yes! Take her now!

But he did not.

He thought quickly instead.

And felt that explosive rush of skin and muscles shifting, features rearranging, as quick as a heartbeat, as natural as breath.

So now he could listen.

Stay close and watch.

And like so many times before, Lucy would never even know.

1.

She hadn't expected the cemetery to look so spooky at this hour of the morning.

Like wandering phantoms, tatters of soft white mist hovered among the graves, and an unnatural quiet smothered the sound of Lucy's footsteps as she made her way to the remote section of the burial grounds. The dead slept deep and undisturbed. Remembered and forgotten alike, they surrounded her on all sides, rotting peacefully to dust.

In the distance, the Wetherly mausoleum came darkly into view, silhouetted against the gloom. As Lucy got nearer, she could see the wrought-iron gates and stone angels that guarded it, and for one unsettling moment, she remembered her dream about Byron and his warning.

"Keep away . . . there's no one in this place."

An icy shudder worked its way up her spine. Hesitating, she dug her hands into her coat pockets and glanced back over her shoulder.

Come on, Lucy, get a grip.

It was easy to imagine eerie whispers and invisible watchers in a creepy place like this—what had she been thinking anyway, coming here so early?

Stop scaring yourself. Nobody here can hurt you.

Giving herself a stern mental shake, she walked over to the front of the tomb. To her surprise, the double gates weren't padlocked as she'd assumed they'd be—in fact, they were standing partway open, one of them creaking rustily as the breeze swung it back and forth.

Heart quickening, Lucy glanced around a second time.

If someone *were* here, they'd be impossible to see, she admitted to herself. Anyone could be hiding close by or far away.

Lucy suppressed another shiver.

Turning in a slow circle, she scanned the graves and headstones, the sepulchres and statues, the trees and shadows and mist. A taste of fear crept into her throat, and she tried to choke it down.

Cautiously, she turned back to the gates.

Taking one in each hand, she eased them open the rest of the way. Cracks had widened along the foundation, and leaves had sifted in over the broken, weathered stones of the floor.

Holding her breath, Lucy walked into the crypt.

She saw the muddy footprints and tufts of clotted hair; the dark, reddish-brown stains smeared along the walls . . .

But she didn't see the figure behind her.

Not till she turned and screamed and stumbled from his arms, trying wildly to fight her way free.

And then she stared up, shocked, into eyes as black and deep as midnight.

"Oh my God," she choked. "Who are you?"

The dark-haired young man gazed coolly back at her.

"Byron's brother," he answered. "Who the hell are *you*?"

2.

He could almost have been Byron.

The likeness was so incredible that for one wild moment Lucy actually glanced around at the walls of the mausoleum, as though Byron himself might have stepped from his burial place to stand before her now.

And yet, in one swift moment of scrutiny, she could see that there were differences. Differences not only obvious, but subtle as well—differences she felt certain of but couldn't totally define. Even in that moment of shock, Lucy sensed a sadness even more complicated than Byron's, and a raw sensitivity far beyond any that Byron had ever shown.

She wanted to look away but was transfixed. At first glance, she'd mistaken his eyes for that same midnight black that Byron's had been, but now that she was closer, she could see they were actually a deep amber color, surrounding unusually large black pupils. The effect of this was a wide, unwavering stare that Lucy found both disturbing and fascinating, and as he held her gaze, she noted that his eyes never blinked.

Lucy guessed him to be about the same height and weight as Byron, with the same lean build. His face was less rugged, his cheekbones every bit as prominent, his nose more slender, his features slightly more delicate. He had a high forehead and low curved brows, the same faint beard shadow along his jaws and chin and upper lip. His perfectly shaped mouth looked both sensuous and seductive; his dark straight hair, parting naturally in the middle, fell to just below his ears.

Weary shadows rimmed his eyes. Shadows like bruises, hollowing his cheeks and accentuating the unnatural ghost-white pallor of his skin. And slashing downward from his left ear to the right side of his chin was a long, jagged scar that seemed very deep and very old.

In this quick instant of observation, two

bizarre thoughts flashed unexpectedly into Lucy's mind.

That he was perhaps the most beautiful young man she'd ever seen in her entire life. And that he and Byron could have been magically superimposed, like two photographs layered together, forming a familiar, yet brand-new, face.

"Byron . . ."

Without even realizing it, she whispered the name. And though the stranger's gaze had seemed to stop time, Lucy jolted back to awareness, realizing that only seconds had passed.

Realizing he wasn't Byron.

This stranger, this bold trespasser standing before her now, wasn't Byron, could never be Byron. Byron was dead, Byron was out of her life forever, Byron had no brother or she would have known, he would have told her. It was all too much—too much to absorb, too much to process—and suddenly Lucy realized that she was having trouble breathing, that her throat was closing up.

"Who are you?" she heard the young man ask again, but his voice was like a dream, and Lucy couldn't answer.

She felt as if she was suffocating. The air in the mausoleum was thick and heavy, settling over her like folds of velvet, crushing her with a sweetness that was almost sickening.

She knew that sweetness.

She'd smelled it before, that cloying fragrance of allure and elusion, but where was it coming from now? It hadn't been in the mausoleum when she'd gotten here—had it? Could she have somehow not realized?

Turning, she looked down at the dark red stains upon the stones, the clotted hair along the floor. Her mind reeled backward, back to the cave and back to her terror. Dark splatters over the ground . . . dark smears trailing back into the tunnel where light couldn't reach . . .

No, it's not the same, she tried to convince herself. This grisly scene has nothing to do with the other, this was just some stray animal, this can be explained.

But she was starting to feel light-headed and confused. Was this the scent of blood? The aftermath of fear? The lingering odor of death?

"What do you want?"

Had he spoken aloud just now? Had she?

12

Lucy put her hands to her temples and tried to concentrate. Bring herself back into focus. He was still staring at her, as though he didn't even notice the sweet, sultry odor enclosing them. What was wrong with him? Surely he could smell it—how could he not smell it?

Yet even as she started to mention it to him, the sweetness was already fading. And then a cold, raw breeze snaked through the tomb and the fragrance vanished completely.

But the young man hadn't gone. The young man hadn't disappeared with the blast of the wind; he was still here, gazing down at her with a frown more curious than threatening.

Brother . . .

The word whispered softly through her head. Once again she wondered if one of them had spoken, or if the thought had simply crept unbidden into her subconscious.

"You didn't know?" His lips were moving now. His voice was deep like Byron's . . . soft like Byron's . . .

Brother . . . of course . . . that would explain the resemblance . . .

"You're not Byron's brother," Lucy said.

13

Her voice was strong with resolve, with a defiance that surprised her. And then came the anger, fierce and possessive, rushing through her like fire. How dare this stranger encroach into Byron's resting place—how dare he claim Byron's name! Her insides were trembling, grief transformed to protective rage, as though she were facing down something evil that had crept onto hallowed ground.

She lifted her chin, fists clenched tightly at her sides. "Byron doesn't have a brother."

"Is that what he told you?" the young man countered. He sounded exhausted, too empty for any sort of emotion.

"Yes, he—"

Lucy stopped, suddenly unsure. What had Byron told her? He'd talked about Katherine and his grandmother, about himself when he was a child.

He'd never said anything about having a brother

But then again, he'd never actually said that he didn't.

Flustered, Lucy gazed back at the stranger. He was leaning a little toward one wall, his left arm pressed close to his side. He must be freezing, she thought, and no wonder, dressed as he was in ragged jeans and T-shirt, scruffy denim jacket and dirty old boots. He'd looked pale before, but now he was even whiter. His skin seemed paperlike, almost translucent, and for the first time she noticed the slight trembling of his hands.

"I don't believe you." Even though you look so much like Byron, even though you sound so much like Byron, even though I wish you were Byron because you've made my heart ache all over again. "Matt would have told me if he'd found you."

"I don't know who you're talking about." He hesitated briefly. "And nobody knows I'm here."

"Then you'd better leave before I call the police."

"That wouldn't be a very smart thing to do."

Backing away, Lucy drew herself to full height. "Are you threatening me?"

"No, I'm just saying—" He broke off, breath catching sharply in his throat, and Lucy watched as he braced himself against the wall and clamped his arm tighter to his side.

"I'm just saying," he continued softly, "that I'm not particularly fond of authority figures, and I wish you wouldn't call them."

Lucy kept her eyes on him. "Why not? Are you in some kind of trouble?"

"That would be a very long story."

"Go ahead. I've got time."

"Not that much time, I'm afraid." One corner of his mouth twisted, though whether from bitterness or amusement, it was hard to tell. "You were close to Byron?"

The question caught Lucy offguard. As she fumbled for an answer, she saw those strange amber eyes glide smoothly down her body, then up again to her face, with an almost suggestive—and calculated—slowness.

"Close?" Cheeks flushing, Lucy did her best to recover. "I was . . . am . . . a friend."

"You must have known him well."

Again Lucy hesitated. "I didn't know him very long. Only a few days."

"That's more than just friendship I see in your eyes."

Startled, she glanced away. She remembered the secret Byron had shared with her—his

16

ability to view people's souls through their eyes. Was this stranger referring to something that only Bryon's brother could have known? Lucy forced herself to look back at him, but his expression revealed nothing.

"You don't know anything about me," she said angrily.

"You might be surprised."

It was a quiet answer, and matter-of-fact, but one that sent a chill through Lucy's heart. It was all she could do to keep her voice level. "What's that supposed to mean?"

His right hand lifted to fend off her question. With growing dismay, Lucy watched a violent shudder work through him, gnawing deep into his muscles. He bent lower, lips tightening, skin like chalk. His eyes squeezed shut, then opened again, seeking her out as though she'd suddenly gone invisible.

"Is Byron really dead?" he murmured.

He was still shivering but trying not to show it, easing himself onto his knees, left arm still clutched to his side. For a panicked moment she wondered if he might be on drugs or out of his mind—maybe even dying. Whatever was wrong with him, he was definitely in no shape to chase her, she decided. Now was her chance to run away, drive off, call for help. He even seemed a little disoriented; with any luck, he might not even notice she'd gone.

But he was between her and the doorway, and Lucy had to get past him. And even though there was enough space to slip by, something held her back. Something about the way he just knelt there, shoulders slumped, head bowed, his dark profile in sharp relief among many, yet seeming so alone . . .

She made a run for it.

With lightning speed he caught her, right arm flinging out, fingers clamping tight around her wrist.

Lucy gasped at the shock. Not just the iciness of his skin or the alarming strength of his grip, but the images that exploded through her brain.

Sweet night—leaves, stars, moonlight patterns—shadows swift on silent feet—dark desires deep as open wounds—wind flowing like blood, streaming like blood, hot wild fountains and rivers of blood—screams from secret places, screams that no one hears, pleasure, pain, and begging screams of terror and surrender . . .

No! Lucy tried to pull free. No more visions! Make them stop!

But the stranger's hand squeezed tighter, sending a chaos of sensations to her very core.

Burning. . .

"Please—"

Burning lungs, burning skin, burning eyes . . .

"Let go!"

Burning like the moon, red just like the moon, burning eyes, burning lips, burning souls.

"Is he?" she heard him ask again. "Is Byron dead?"

Lucy felt the walls sway around her, the stones shift beneath her feet. For one brief second the young man's eyes actually seemed to change color, black and amber fusing together in a liquid, luminous glow—yet she convinced herself it was only a trick of her own unshed tears. She tried to answer him—wanted to answer him—but her thoughts were all muddled, and she was so hot, and he was holding her so tight . . . so tight . . .

"Yes." Don't make me say it—I can't bear to say it! "Yes! He's dead!"

"You're sure?"

Memories stabbed through her head, pierced through her heart. "If you were really his brother, you wouldn't be asking me these questions! If you were really his brother, you'd already know—"

"How . . . long?"

He could barely gasp out the words. There was sweat along his brow and upper lip, though his breath hung like frost in the air. Lucy felt sick with both sympathy and dread.

"What is it?" she begged him. "What's wrong?"

"How long ago?"

Her mind raced feverishly, trying to find the answer. How long had it been since Byron died? Already much too long. Forever. A heart-breaking eternity.

"Days?" Strength was draining from his fingers; he fumbled for a tighter grasp. "Weeks?"

"Weeks. A couple of weeks—"

"Was there a funeral?"

"Yes."

"A service? A special service?"

"Some kind of service, yes—"

"A casket?"

As hard as she tried to prevent them, more unwanted memories flooded in. The gloomy day, the weeping crowd of mourners. The priest in black, the flowers and personal keepsakes arranged upon the coffin. She couldn't hold back tears any longer. They ran down her cheeks and dripped on the hand that held her.

"And there's no mistake?" he persisted. "There couldn't possibly be some mistake? You're absolutely sure he's dead?"

"I . . . " Sobs rose into her throat, though she stubbornly fought them down. "I was with him when he died."

His fingers slid from her arm. As Lucy stepped away and began rubbing circulation back into her wrist, she heard the hollow sound of his whisper.

"So . . . it's true, then."

Free to escape now, Lucy realized she couldn't. Something about the tonelessness of his voice, the defeated sag of his shoulders, held her there in a conflict of emotions. She watched in silence as he eased himself back against the wall, legs splayed in front of him, head bent to his chest. His right hand lifted in slow motion, fingers gliding back through his tangled mane of hair.

"Bryon." Had he choked just then? Laughed? Sobbed? His voice was so faint, Lucy could barely hear. "Damn you, Byron . . . "

Her heart caught at the words. She didn't know what to do. What to say. What to think or even believe. Something inside her felt the need to comfort him; something inside her still sensed a threat. Finally, in spite of herself, she took a cautious step toward him and reached out for his shoulder.

"After all this time," he murmured.

Lucy stopped, hand poised midair. "What?" she asked him gently.

He lifted his head and rested it back against the wall. He wasn't looking at her anymore. In truth, he didn't even seem to realize she was there.

"After all this time," he murmured again. "And now I'm too late."